WINGS OF SPIRIT

G. BAILEY

CONTENTS

Created with Vellum

MORE BOOKS BY G. BAILEY

HER GUARDIANS SERIES

HER FATE SERIES

PROTECTED BY DRAGONS SERIES

LOST TIME ACADEMY SERIES

THE DEMON ACADEMY SERIES

DARK ANGEL ACADEMY SERIES

SHADOWBORN ACADEMY SERIES

DARK FAE PARANORMAL PRISON SERIES

SAVED BY PIRATES SERIES

THE MARKED SERIES

HOLLY OAK ACADEMY SERIES

THE ALPHA BROTHERS SERIES

A DEMON'S FALL SERIES

THE FAMILIAR EMPIRE SERIES

FROM THE STARS SERIES

THE FOREST PACK SERIES

THE SECRET GODS PRISON SERIES

THE REJECTED MATE SERIES

FALL MOUNTAIN SHIFTERS SERIES

ROYAL REAPERS ACADEMY SERIES

THE EVERLASTING CURSE SERIES

THE MOON ALPHA SERIES

DESCRIPTION

Three secrets. Two fights. And one broken curse.

Isola is finally back in Dragca, but nothing is the same when she is hunted and betrayed by everyone she meets. With one of her dragon guards fighting for his life, time is running out.

When the seers come to her aid, lies and blood are their price. With two battles on her hands, one for their freedom and one for her dragon guards, Isola has a lot to fight for . . . and a lot to lose.

The dragon guard curse must be broken, for fire has finally fallen for ice . . . but is death the final price?

This story follows the Her Guardian Universe from a new point of view.

For all those who fight the impossible and win.

PROLOGUE

No! I scream in my dragon's head as we fall through the trees and land on the ground, his claws finally coming free of my wings, so I can move. I shoot ice onto his wings as he tries to fly and keep shooting it until his entire dragon is frozen to the ground. His dragon's eyes almost dead as I stare at him encased in the ice. I look up, not seeing Thorne or any other dragons flying around.

"It has been a long time, Isola, don't you think?" Tatarina's cold, detached-sounding voice says from behind me, and my dragon turns to roar at her. I feel down my wings, knowing the damage to them is too much, and I won't be able to fly out of here for a bit.

There is only one thing we can do, even if it makes me vulnerable.

Let me take over? I ask my dragon, who doesn't hesitate as we shift back. I stand up straight, keeping my head high as I face Tatarina. She stands still like a ghost; her dark, nearly black hair blowing in the wind is the only movement. Her eyes are completely black, and they match the dark glow her skin now has. I look over as a woman moves out from the shadows of the trees, making me take a step back.

"Bu-but, I killed you!" I gasp as Esmeralda stands by her sister's side, smiling widely with her blood-red lips. Her eyes are now as red as her hair, and her pale skin is littered with black veins.

"Death was not my ending," Esmeralda replies, her voice croaking and broken in places. Her head twitches as she speaks, and Tatarina places her hand on her sister's arm.

"I will remember to chop your head off next time," I sneer. "Just to be sure."

"There will not be a next time, for this is *your* ending, Isola," Tatarina says, holding her hands out at her sides. "You are all alone, and I am queen. Is this what you always thought would happen?"

"Isola, we need to take a break," Melody gently urges, as I step over another fallen branch and pause, looking back. Melody is resting against a tree, looking breathless and tired, but watching me. I feel like crap, too, but I know we can't just rest now. Resting could mean death, and I don't want to risk it. Bee strokes my cheek from where she sits on my shoulder, making me turn my head to stare into her green eyes. I can almost feel her sadness like it's my own.

"Your sister is right, we need to stop. We have been walking for about ten hours, I believe," Dagan says quietly, walking to my side. I automatically step away from him, shaking my head as I look at Korbin. His arms are around Thorne's and Elias's shoulders, and he is struggling to stand up as they all wait for me to say something. I know he needs to rest, but we need to get out of this damn forest and find somewhere safe.

"We can't, look at him," I wave a hand at Korbin. The purple lines of the poison are crawling up his pale face, and he can barely hold his head up. He is sweaty, pale, and looks on the verge of death. The poison is killing him.

"Isola, we are stopping. Korbin needs to rest, too," Dagan says, nodding his head at Thorne and Elias who carefully set Korbin down next to a tree. He is barely conscious, and not strong enough to even hold his head up. "We are all worried. I get that, but we need to rest. We won't stop long. I promise."

I turn to Dagan, nodding in acceptance before walking over to Korbin and sitting next to him. I place my hand on his forehead, feeling how burning hot he is, and his green eyes pop open, a little smirk appearing on his lips.

"You make a sexy nurse, doll," he tells me, and I chuckle, shaking my head. "I like hearing you laugh," he coughs on his words, and I see blood on his hand even as he tries to hide it from me as he lowers his hand to his side.

"I like hearing you awake and talking. Do you want some water?" I ask him, clearing my throat as I try to speak through the fear I'm feeling. He nods, and I pull the small water bottle out of the bag that Melody brought with her. We have pretty much emptied it already. There wasn't much in there to start with, but it's better than nothing. We don't have a lot of water left now, but we have to find a village soon, and we can re-stock. I open the plastic bottle, holding it to his lips and helping him drink. Before I put the bottle back, I take a long drink for myself. I rest the bag on the ground near Korbin. I look up as Bee flies off my shoulder, landing on Korbin's lap and smiling up at him. She is growing; she even looks bigger than when I first saw her again.

"Dying," Bee says, pointing a tiny hand at his stomach, and Korbin laughs, even though it makes him cough.

"Thanks for telling me that, Bee. I think I know, though, and don't need a reminder," he says playfully, and Bee shrugs, looking over at me with worry in her eyes.

"Food?" she asks, holding out a hand.

"We don't have any food left, I'm sorry. There is water . . ." I say, and she sighs dramatically, flying up past us and sitting on a branch hanging over Korbin. She lies down, her long green hair blowing in the wind, and I think she is going to sleep, but who knows. She hasn't talked to anyone much on the walk here. Well, none of us have really spoken, and I think it's about time that changed. It's been years since I was last in Dragca, and I'm worried what I'm going to find when we get out of this forest. I look back at Korbin, seeing his eyes are closed and light sounds of snoring are coming from his chest. I end up just watching his chest move for a while. The movement reminds me that he is alive, and we still have time to save him. A branch cracks behind me, and I turn to see Elias standing there. His hair is messy, and his dark-blue eyes don't have that glow to them anymore. He looks crushed, just like all my dragon guards have since we got here. Since they lost their dragons because of me. I struggle to swallow the guilt I feel as I look at Elias.

"We are all going to sleep for a bit, and I'm on first watch. Get some rest," he says.

"I can't sleep," I say, frustrated, and stand up. I don't want to sleep, because all I can think about is what happened when I last let myself be vulnerable. How I couldn't stop him and needed someone to save me. I can't sleep because I'm scared I'll wake up and Korbin will be gone. He needs me. Sleep is the last thing on my mind, but I can't make the words leave my lips that I want to tell Elias. I look over to see Dagan making a fire, and the simple, normal act makes me relax a little. Reminds me that I'm safe, for now anyway. I look away to see Melody is resting against another tree, her hood covering her face, and Thorne is standing not far from us, watching the forest.

"You should try," Elias says gently, moving to touch my arm, but stopping as I flinch.

"I'm sorry, it's not you," I blurt out my excuse. I can't believe I just quoted every terrible clichéd movie quote as someone gets dumped. Not that I'm dumping Elias. I literally can't as we share blood. We share a bond, and I don't want to dump him anyway. I just feel scared to let him touch me, to let him hold me and tell me this is all okay when it's so far from okay. I can still feel Michael's hands on me, still feel how weak I felt and how powerless.

"It's him, I know. When you're ready, I will always be waiting," he tells me, and I nod. I want to reach out and hold his hand, but I just can't. I almost hate myself for it when I see the longing in his eyes.

"It's impossible to make you walk away, isn't it?" I slightly tease him.

"You know it," he smirks.

I walk over to Thorne, stopping at his side. He doesn't move, doesn't speak for a long time as I follow his gaze through the forest. It's silent and almost peaceful.

"What has changed in Dragca while I've been gone? I need to know what your mother has done," I ask quietly, and Thorne finally looks over at me, his pale-blue eyes still so hauntingly open to me. I can see what he feels, almost guess exactly what he is thinking, just by looking into them. He doesn't hide anything from me, but it's still not enough for me to trust him again. Saving me wasn't enough for me to trust him with my heart again, but I know I can't let him walk away from me yet, either. His pale-blond hair moves around his face in the wind, and his cloak floats just behind him as we watch each other. *I wonder what he thinks as he looks at me?* Does he see a scared princess, or someone else? Someone that is worth all of this. He still wears the royal cloak, the ice and fire dragons embroidered into it. It's just a reminder of what happened to get us to this point. I hate that I can't trust him, and I hate that it hurts my heart every time I think of our past.

"A lot," he answers. Two words are not enough to explain everything I need to know. I'm tired of this; I won't settle for these non-answers anymore. How am I meant to save Dragca, convince the seers I'm their queen, and somehow get my dragon guard their dragons back when they treat me like a clueless girl?

"Simple answers are not enough right now. Tell me everything, Thorne. I will never trust you, never accomplish all I'm meant to, if you don't tell me what I need to know. I'm not the same girl you met at Dragca Academy, the girl who didn't know what she wanted or who she was . . . I am Isola Dragice, and I want to know what has happened to *my* world," I demand, getting frustrated with him as he still silently watches me. I feel Dagan's approach, just before he steps to my side and places his arm around my waist. I don't know why I can let Dagan touch me, hold me. Maybe it's just because he doesn't ask permission to hold or support me. He just does, and once I'm near him, I don't want to pull away.

"Why don't we all sit by the fire and discuss this? There are things we haven't had a chance to tell the princess, also," Dagan asks Thorne as he rolls his lip ring in typical Dagan fashion. Thorne doesn't seem to notice as he seems more focused on my proximity to Dagan than listening to him.

"Like what?" I ask Dagan, wondering what he could possibly be talking about.

"Your father gave us a mission before he died, before we even met you. A mission based on a prophecy that no one other than the old king knew about," Dagan says, keeping his light-blue eyes locked on mine. I try to hold my dragon's growl in as I move out of Dagan's arms and feel ice on my fingertips as I get angry.

Too many secrets, my dragon whispers in my mind, and I couldn't agree with her more.

"Tell me everything, and no one leaves out any secrets this time," I demand, shooting a fierce look at both Dagan and Thorne before stepping away and walking over to the fire.

"Start from the beginning," I say, standing with my arms crossed as Dagan, Elias, and Thorne walk to the fire, crowding in close to me. It's strange to see them all together like this; my dragon guards who I've been falling for and the dragon guard that has been haunting my dreams. I can't stop myself from stealing glances at Thorne every so often because the dreams didn't do him justice. I forgot what it was like to be near him, to have that inexplicable connection I feel. A connection that makes me forget about his betrayal, which I never want to do. Melody looks up from the tree she is resting against, listening in as her blue eyes lock on mine. My sister has yet to say much, though she's always watching me every time I look at her. I have a feeling she is hiding things from us, but calling her out on it won't work. I imagine she is as stubborn as I can be. I hear a cough, and I look over to find Korbin sleeping, chest heaving. He sounds like he's in pain, and it's worrying me. This isn't Earth, I can't just take him to a doctor and demand they fix him. We need a healer that doesn't work for the new queen. It's like looking for a needle in a haystack, but with that haystack on fire. I can't even bring myself to acknowledge that I might lose Korbin, not with how I feel for him. I love him, the pain I feel every time I look at him confirming it.

"Maybe you should start," Elias suggests, giving Dagan a pointed look before his dark eyes drift back to me. Elias's black hair is messy, and he looks tired, yet still so incredibly hot. It's easy to get lost in my thoughts when I look at Elias, and the smirk on his lips lets me know he knows what I'm thinking.

"No, Korbin should be the one telling this to Isola as he started it all, but here we go," Dagan says, clearing his throat and not looking my way as he starts to speak. "Korbin's parents were both close to the king, and your father asked them to find three dragon guards he could trust implicitly. Of course, they chose their son, and Korbin asked us, trusting only us to keep a secret," he says, pausing to look at Korbin, and Elias takes over.

"We were brought to the king, and the first words he said were, 'The ones that come when called, will fall for ice. When fire falls for ice, darkness will have its price.'" I muse over his words, completely confused. *Why would my father say that?*

"I heard about the lost prophecy from my mother, but she never told me what it said. I think she feared it, hated it maybe," Thorne admits, and we all look at him for a second. If his mother fears this prophecy, we need to know everything about it. Thorne keeps his eyes locked on mine for only a minute, and I see so much guilt. It reminds me that I still need to tell him what Melody showed me, what his mother has done. I just need to find time alone with him. He shouldn't have an audience when he learns the truth.

"What is it? What else did it say, and who made it?" I rapidly ask questions as the cold wind blows against all of us, and Dagan holds his hands over the fire, warming them up as he answers.

"He didn't share the full prophecy with us. Only that single sentence and one other thing, before demanding that we meet him at Dragca Academy in two weeks when you were to return to Dragca. He told us to stay quiet and follow you," he tells me. I stay silent for a while, just staring at the fire. My father was keeping more secrets from me, and it doesn't even surprise me anymore. I don't know how he expected me to take the throne when it was built on so many lies. I look over at Melody, who doesn't seem shocked. She is a prime example of those lies.

"Tell me?" I look towards Dagan and ask carefully.

"He told us that ice cannot rule anymore, that ice and fire must find balance. That light and dark must find their way to survive, together. He said that we would be crucial in the war that was coming. A war that will destroy Dragca, destroy Earth, and anything light or dark in our worlds unless we stand in its way. Unless we change what everyone has always known," Dagan says, and there's a tense silence between us all as I look into the fire, trying to collect my thoughts before I reply to them. My father knew something, something bad, and he sent my guards to me. He knew they would fall for me, like I would fall for them, but why didn't he say anything to me? I look over at Melody, who just pulls her hood back up, hiding her face in darkness and not saying a word. I bet my sister knows more than she is admitting right now.

"So, let me get this straight. We have four dragon guards who don't have their dragons, one of which is injured and dying. One seer who doesn't talk to us, and one accident prone princess that is supposed to be dead. . . *and* we have to save two worlds?" I blurt out. *Nope, sorry, we are all going to die.*

"You forgot Bee," Thorne points out, and looks at me seriously. "You are not just some accident-prone princess who is powerless. You can control light magic, the most powerful magic known to Dragca. You are an ice dragon, and you can fight. Don't count yourself out just yet," he says. At least he admits I have some faults like tripping over my own feet sometimes, rather than ignoring them.

"I don't know how to *use* light magic, and Bee isn't old enough to tell me," I say as an excuse, but even my voice falters with my weak retort. Honestly, I haven't thought about light magic. I have no idea what it can do. I don't know what dark magic can do either, and the fear of both is making me not want to find out.

"Have you tried asking her? She isn't a baby anymore," Thorne points out.

"You still haven't told me what has happened in Dragca since I've been gone," I counter, because I don't want to admit I haven't asked Bee about it, and I'm not sure how to. Light and dark magic are unpredictable, and that's the last thing we need right now.

"Remember that my mother isn't evil, she really isn't, so don't you all look at me like you feel sorry for me. I don't agree with what my mother has done, and I'll admit the power has gone to her head, but there is still good in her. I only need to get close enough to talk some reason into her. She will stop this and place Isola on the throne. I'm sure of it," Thorne insists, and I briefly glance at Dagan who shakes his head in exasperation. This isn't the time to disagree with him, and Thorne keeps talking before I can even think of replying, anyway. "My mother has destroyed the councils. Esmeralda killed the selected that ruled them and placed one ruler she trusts in each of the main towns. My mother has started a culling for new dragon guards, making them join her without giving them any choice. I don't know too much about how she is forcing them to join, but the dragon guard is growing far larger than it's ever been," he admits to us, and I close my hands into fists in anger.

"She is forcing them to join the guard? Making them curse themselves?" I gasp in shock. My father never did that. Anyone can join the dragon guard, but it was always a choice, and they knew the price. Forcing them . . . it sends shivers of disgust down my spine. No queen should force her people to do that. Ruling with fear is not ruling at all. It's a path to destruction.

"The people don't have a choice. She threatens their families if they don't join . . . or kills them outright. I met a few in the dungeons that she had imprisoned for refusing to join her," Dagan tells me, reminding me they spent the last two years trapped in the dungeons. They must know some things that could help us. It reminds me that I still haven't thanked Thorne for keeping them alive, for setting them free, and helping Bee and Melody. There is a lot I haven't thanked him for, but I just don't trust myself not to blurt out a load of other things I'm thinking when we are alone.

"What else?" I ask tentatively, almost not wanting to hear the answer. The guilty look in Thorne's eyes lets me know there is more to this story.

"She has raised taxes, cut down on food provisions, and gained total control over Dragca with fear," Elias answers instead, and Thorne glares at him.

"You make it sound worse than it is. She only did that to feed the army, and she offered anyone who wants to join a place there, with their families protected," Thorne snaps back.

"Every dragon would rather die than join the dragon guard and curse their whole family. Your mother gave them no choice," Elias spits out.

"Enough!" I shout at them, and they both stop instantly, turning to me. "We cannot fight amongst ourselves like this, not when Korbin needs us to find him help, and we have true enemies everywhere."

"The princess is right, but my mother is not completely evil," Thorne contends, and walks away from us all. I want to follow him, tell him everything I know about his mother and that he is wrong about her, but I don't.

"It is not yet time, sister," Melody's voice drifts over to me, but I still watch Thorne as I reply.

"I know."

THREE

"I finally know where we are," Dagan says, and I stop, looking back at him as he helps Thorne hold up Korbin. Thorne has a royal cloak on now, covering up his eyes and hair, much like I do. We both stand out way too much otherwise. The only difference, I have my ice power, and he doesn't. It would be a death sentence if anyone spotted Thorne. Elias and Melody are behind them, watching their backs as I stay in front. As Melody and I are the only ones with any powers currently, it's smart to have us at the front and the back. I follow Dagan's gaze to our left, where there is a row of trees and a path in the middle of them. The trees have dragons engraved down the trunk, painted in red.

"Where are we?" I ask, curious. I don't see any towns, but the path looks well worn.

"Where we first met you, kitty cat," Dagan says playfully, but I can see the pain in his eyes when he looks at me. His old home, where he lost his mum, which, no doubt, holds some awful memories for them. I glance around Dagan to Elias, who looks tense, staring at the ground. Of all the places we could have ventured to, it had to be their old home.

"Which town is it?" Melody asks.

"Mesmoia," Elias answers gruffly.

"Perfect! Mesmoia is only two days away from where the seers are hiding, and where I saw us meeting them," Melody answers happily. She opens her bag up, and Bee flies off my shoulder straight into it, knowing she has to hide for now.

"But we still need to get through the town without anyone recognising us and get help for Korbin," I tell Melody firmly. She looks at Korbin, and then nods.

"We don't really have the time, but he won't make it to the seers like this. I guess we have no choice," Melody states, looking away from us all as she puts her bag back on.

"I know someone in Mesmoia that might hide us. If he is still alive, anyway," Dagan tells me.

"Can he be trusted?" I ask.

"No idea. He was a friend of our mentor growing up. I don't want to trust him, but we don't really have much of a choice," Dagan says, looking down at Korbin, who they are just dragging along the floor at this point. He isn't conscious, and his breathing is shallow.

"Let's just go. Like you said, we don't have a choice because I refuse to let him die. We risk this for Korbin, he's worth it," I say, making my mind up and knowing they feel the same when none of them disagree with me. This could be Korbin's only chance, and there is no way I'm not taking it. Elias catches up to my side as we get to the row of trees, and we start walking down the path. I pull the hood of my coat up, hiding my blonde hair and knowing I need to keep my eyes on the ground when we enter the village.

"How are you?" Elias prods quietly, his hand brushing mine with every step. He doesn't push to hold my hand, but the little contact feels like he needs it.

"Fine," I answer quickly.

"Tut, tut, naughty princess. You know I don't like lies," Elias calls me out on my crap, and I sigh, looking back at Korbin and then to Elias.

"I'm worried, scared, and I can't think of anything other than saving Korbin right now. My problems can wait," I explain, and he gives me a dark look, full of understanding. I love that with Elias, he just gets what I mean. He knows what I'm feeling like he can feel it himself. And that one kiss with him, just stays on repeat at the back of my mind. I find myself staring at his lips, and then I don't know what happens. I just freeze, pulled into a memory of being defenseless on that bed in Michael's house, and ice starts dripping from my hands.

Safe. Mine keep us safe, my dragon comforts me, and I try to shake the panic off.

"When you're ready to talk about it, let me in. I was brought up in a whorehouse, and it wasn't a pleasant childhood. I might be easier to talk to, than just holding it all in that pretty mind of yours," he says, not looking my way as he speaks. It's hard for him, too, I can feel that. I think my blood bond with them is making my emotions more connected with theirs, and I need to find out more about blood bonds. I know it means we can find each other, no matter where, and we can feel great emotion or physical pain. It's not the same as a mating bond, that bond is far more.

"Why didn't your mum move you out of the whorehouse? Let you live anywhere else?"

"She couldn't afford to after our dad left her. She wasn't always a whore, we know that. It was only the last three years of her life she was in there with us. We were safe, most of the time anyway, but we saw things no kid ever should," he admits, and I only pause for a brief moment before I grab his hand, linking our fingers.

"Your dad left?"

"Yeah, my mum said he left her for another dragon and that was the end of it. He must have been a dragon guard, because we are, but we don't know much else. If I ever see him, I'm going to kill him," he tells me firmly, and I feel his hand warm up in mine. Even though he doesn't have his dragon, his hand can still burn hot. I call my ice to my hand, just to cool it down, and it melts instantly.

"Life seems to like making us stronger before it allows us to be happy," I say, and he squeezes my hand.

"I'm happy with you, even in these little moments I manage to steal. I know you're hurting, and that's on me. Once again, I didn't protect you, and I can't begin to tell you how much I regret it," he says, almost gently, but there is so much anger in his voice that he just can't hide from me. I wish I felt angry, and not just scared of a human. Of what could have happened.

"He was a human, and I still wasn't strong enough to stop him. If Thorne . . ." I stop, feeling hot tears streaming down my face as I talk about what happened for the first time, and I can't even look at Elias.

"It's no secret I dislike Thorne. I think he has his own motives for everything he does and loves no one but himself and his mother. But when I saw him walking through the door with you in his arms, he was so angry, so furious that anyone had tried to hurt you. He was destroyed with his anger and pain for you. I will always owe him for saving you, and I believe he would do anything to keep you alive," Elias tells me, making my eyes drift over to Thorne for a moment. He is watching me, but I can only see his blue eyes as he is hidden in his cloak.

"I still don't trust him. Betrayal changes every-thing, particularly anything we once had," I say.

"You still don't get what I'm trying to tell you, princess," Elias says, almost teasingly.

"Explain then," I respond, smiling a little.

"Thorne has betrayed everyone that is close to him. His mother. His aunt. You. Everyone . . . but it was *you* he came back for. It was you from the very start, and that's why you should let him, and us, protect you. What happened on Earth, it was all of our fault. I remember feeling like Michael was a threat, and if I had known who I was, I would have killed him before he ever had a chance to lay a finger on you," Elias growls out.

"He didn't . . . you know. Thorne killed him just before he could . . ." I let my voice trail off because I can't say the word. I have to remember I'm in Dragca, not Earth, and that I'm safe from Michael. I don't need to worry or panic. Everything is going to be okay.

"I'm glad to know that, but don't let him win. He is just a bug, a bug your dragon guard stomped on, so you can rise above him. In ten years, a thousand, no one will remember him, but Dragca will always remember you. No matter what happens, they will know you fight for Dragca, for them," Elias firmly tells me, and I nod, agreeing with him as his words fill me with pride. I'm not the only one that will be remembered if I get my way. Elias, Dagan, Korbin, and Thorne should be, too. I ignore the little whisper that drifts in my head, the thought that they will be remembered as my mates.

Minnnee . . . my dragon demands, and her urge to shift and fly brushes against my mind.

It isn't safe. Soon, trust me.

Soon, I want revenge, she growls, before settling down. I focus back on Elias, who is watching my eyes closely.

"I love seeing your sexy eyes shift. They are stunning," he tells me.

"I miss seeing yours, it's like I can feel the emptiness of your dragon," I tell him honestly.

"The last thing I heard my dragon tell me, was to protect you. That you are his," he says softly. "He is happy with the choice I made. He never argued once as I stepped into the portal and said goodbye."

"I don't remember much about Mesmoia as a child, what is the town like?" I ask, needing to change the subject. Elias nods his head in front of me, just as we walk over a small hill.

"Why don't you see for yourself?"

FOUR

ISOLA

I stand still, staring at the massive town of Mesmoia and taking in the beauty of it. I don't remember it being beautiful like this, but then, I was so young when I was last here. It is a town full of blue-slate buildings, a massive clock tower in the center, and a wall surrounding the town that is made of dark blue stone, with five large defence towers in the corners with bright blue fires on the tops of them. Seeing the fires, reminds me of my mum taking me here all those years ago. She loved the fire and how its blue light can be seen from our castle. I look back, seeing there is only one way in and one way out, through the large gates I can barely see from here. I look up as three fire dragons shoot across the sky, flying towards the entrance and shifting back.

"You can't fly in or out of the town. In each tower, there is a seer orb, and it has magic that protects Mesmoia," Melody explains as she stops at my side. "Much like my own orb, it needs a seer to re-fill it with magic every few months. I doubt Mesmoia will have its protection for much longer now that the seers aren't on the side of the throne."

"Amazing, and that might be good for us if we need a quick escape at some point," I say, still staring at the town. There is a surprising amount of trees and large bushes full of flowers all around it, making the town seem more alive than I expected.

"Isola, make sure you keep your hood up, and don't look directly at anyone. You, too, Thorne. You're both too easily recognisable," Melody tells me firmly, just as Korbin coughs, and blood drips down his cheek as I run to him. I wipe the blood off his chin with my sleeve, and tilt his head up, seeing how completely out of it he looks. He doesn't even seem to notice me in front of him, and the purple lines are now covering his face, his neck, and I bet, everywhere else. *How long until the poison kills him?*

"We don't have time, Korbin doesn't have time. Let's hope your friend can help us, or I'm freezing the whole goddamn town until someone does," I say, keeping my voice calm despite the fury flowing through me as I let Korbin rest his head down again. I turn around, walking straight down the path towards Mesmoia. Melody catches up to my side, and Dagan stays on my other as Elias swaps places with him to hold Korbin up. We walk as fast as we can down the hill and come to a group of people that are walking towards the entrance. There are five of them, all in ragged clothes, and they are pulling a cart behind them that has two children on it who don't look in any better of a state. They both have dark-red hair, and one of them sits up to stare at me, pushing her messy hair over her shoulder. I look away, but I know we are too close to let her see me. The kid might have seen my eyes, or even a little bit of my hair. Or I might be paranoid... who knows?

"Come here, kitty cat," Dagan holds an arm out for me, and I quickly realise he wants to hold me close to keep me hidden. I step closer, letting him slide an arm around my waist, and I bend my head close to his chest, breathing in his smoky scent. I keep looking to the side as we walk behind the people and their cart, the children still watching us.

"Guards," Dagan whispers close to me, his lips gently brushing the tip of my ear, and I inch my hand to his sword on instinct. I know I can pull it out and attack anyone to get us a distraction to escape. I briefly look up after I feel us starting to walk on stone to see five dragon guards at the gate. They watch us all for a second before another guard walks over to them, and they get distracted talking to each other. I look away just in case I catch any of their gazes, and, thankfully, none of them stop us as we walk straight into the town and join the crowds of people. I lift my head, still keeping close to Dagan's side as I look around. Dozens of people surround us, a mixture of red, black, and brown-haired dragons. Some dragon guards are in their dragon leather, and nearly everyone else has cloaks on, covering themselves up. I spot people huddled together on the ground near a building, begging for food or money, but people walk past them like they aren't even there. The cracked blue-stone path we walk down leads to the clock tower right in the middle of town. The tower is surrounded by little stalls selling foods, powders, clothing, and many other things. There is so much colour, so much life . . . it's amazing and nothing like any human town I've ever seen.

"This way," Dagan pulls at my waist, leading me and the others past all the stalls. We get to an alleyway behind the tower that looks dark, and Dagan walks us down it. We get to the other end which opens up into a quieter part of Mesmoia, and there is a water fountain. I pause, remembering this place as I stare at the stone dragon, the water shooting out of its mouth and spraying into the fountain. The water isn't blue like Earth, it's more of a purple colour. I know humans can't drink the water here; it would kill them and has done so many times. Dragca isn't made for humans, I guess.

"I met you and Elias right here, didn't I?" I ask Dagan, and he nods, making me walk past it and over to a row of small, blue-stone houses like he can't stand for me to stare at where we met for too long. "What's the rush?"

"We need to get inside, but yes," Dagan says, but he doesn't seem to want to linger here for long. Not that I can blame him. Dagan walks us to the house on the very end, with a white door and a dragon-shaped silver knocker, which he knocks a few times. We all wait for what seems like a long time, but is likely only seconds, before the door is pulled open, and an old man stands in front of us. The man has long grey hair plaited in one long plait, and brown trousers, with a brown cloak covering his white shirt underneath. The cloak has a silver dragon crest, my father's crest. My family's crest. It almost hurts to see it, a reminder of how that crest doesn't symbolise the throne anymore. He looks between us all slowly, before scrutinizing me, pausing at Thorne, and his eyes landing on Dagan with a long suffering sigh.

"You bring trouble to my door, boy," the old man states tightly, tipping his head at me.

"Darth, I wouldn't come unless I had nowhere else. Korbin is dying, we need help," Dagan tells him, and he looks over at Korbin, pausing.

"Is that Janiya and Phelan's kid?" Darth asks, seeming curious as he squints his eyes. "They have been looking for him. There's a big reward for his safe return."

"Yes, and you can have the reward, if you help us," Elias says firmly, and Darth steps back, holding the door open.

"You best get him in here then, boy, and the princess, too. We don't allow royalty to stand outside in the cold in this house. My wife would be turning in her grave if I allowed that," Darth mutters, ushering us into his house. I walk in after Dagan, and Melody follows.

"Take him to a bed upstairs," Darth says. We wait as Thorne and Elias carry Korbin into the house and take him straight up the stairs. Darth closes the door behind them, mumbling something under his breath that I don't quite manage to catch. The house is all one massive room downstairs as I look around. The back of the room is the kitchen, with a large fireplace, and then there is the lounge, with two ratty brown sofas and a worn-down rug. There are hole-filled curtains on the windows, which Dagan goes around and closes, so the only light is from the fireplace.

"Now, kid, you'd best start telling me the story of what happened while I find my medicine box," Darth grouses, heading for the kitchen.

"You're a healer?" I ask as he opens a cupboard and starts pulling random pieces of paper, old unrecognizable junk, and some saucepans out. I watch as he chucks them on the floor one by one, making a huge mess. I briefly look at Dagan and Melody, who are watching Darth like I am, wondering why he has so much junk as Darth finally answers me.

"Back in the old days, yes. I worked for your father as a royal healer, until I got too old," he deeply chuckles.

"That's how you knew who I am?" I ponder.

"No, I saw your eyes. They are the mirror image

of your mother's, that's how I knew. That's how anyone would recognise you. You should hide those eyes, princess Isola. Then again, it's much like how I knew one of your guards is the son of the current queen. He has her eyes also, well, before the darkness spread into them," he tells us, never pausing as he moves to another cupboard and starts chucking things out of that one, too.

"You knew my mother when she was younger?" Thorne asks, walking down the stairs having clearly overheard our conversation.

"I knew both of your mothers as children, when they were friends, before jealousy got involved and darkness entered Tatarina's heart. We all watched as your father chose your mother over Tatarina, which was the start of her heart being destroyed with darkness," he pauses to look back at us, noticing our shock. "Such a shame, she was so young for darkness to take its hold, but then she was weak."

"Lies! My mother didn't know the queen, they weren't friends!" Thorne exclaims, and I place my hand on his shoulder on instinct; a need to comfort him, and his eyes flash to my hand before he looks up.

"It makes sense. They were the last ice princesses, and there was only my father they could marry. They would have made them all grow up together, like my father did with me and Jace. That's where he must have gotten the idea from in the first place," I say gently, and Thorne nods, anger in his eyes as he stares down at me.

"She lied to me then. My mother said she never met the queen, not once," he growls.

"You mother lied about a lot of things, you silly boy," Darth chuckles, and Thorne pulls away from me, storming out the door as Darth still laughs. "So much anger, if he doesn't control it, he will end up as bitter as his mother."

"No, he won't," I snap.

"Ah, I see. He belongs to you . . . well, you should tell him the truth. Lies do not make a relationship, they only destroy it," Darth tells me. "Ah, here it is." I watch as he pulls a big box out of the back of the cupboard, holding it up just as Elias runs down the stairs.

"Something's wrong, Korbin needs help! Now!" Elias shouts out, and we all run up the stairs with Darth following. My heart pounds, feeling like it could be destroyed at any second if I lose Korbin.

CHAPTER
FIVE
ISOLA

"**M**ove," Darth pushes Elias out of the way in the hallway, opening the first door to the right and entering the dimly lit room. I follow Elias in, seeing Darth holding Korbin down on the bed by his shoulders as his whole body shakes. Korbin's eyes are rolled back, blood drips from the corner of his mouth, and when I hear him cry my name in pain, I nearly fall to my knees with panic.

"Oh god," I whisper, not feeling attached to my own body as I mentally pray Korbin will make it through this. I can't lose him. I just can't. I don't notice the ice spreading under my feet until Elias nearly slips on it as he rushes into the room. Darth opens the big box he placed on the floor, pulling out a small blue bottle that has white liquid inside. He gets a needle, extracting the liquid. I feel two hands on my shoulders, one is Dagan and the other is Melody, I instinctively know from the way my dragon relaxes a tad at their touch. Darth rubs his face, looking over at us and back at Korbin after a moment.

"Show me where he was poisoned, girl. Elias, hold him down," he orders.

"Can we do anything?" Dagan asks.

"You and the seer girl, go and get hot water from the middle of town. There is gold on the fireplace in the pot, you can pay me back later," Darth tells us, and I rush forward at the same time Elias does. I hear the others rush down the stairs in the background, but I can't focus on them as I watch Elias get closer to Korbin. I know they aren't as close as Dagan is to Kor, but I can see the worry flash across Elias's eyes when he briefly glances at me. Elias holds his shoulders firmly, as I lift Korbin's shirt up and try not to feel sick at the awful smell coming from the now black cut on his stomach. The lines are crawling from the cut, all over his chest and spreading in every direction. Some are massive purple lines and others are tiny little ones.

"Oh mighty. We have work to do," Darth almost

chuckles, like a crazy person, before slamming the needle straight into the cut without pausing once. Korbin calls out my name several times, and I grasp his hand, not knowing what else I can do. Korbin gradually stops shaking, settling down but still out of it as Darth pulls the needle out and places it on the side.

"He needs blood and a bond made, or he dies," Darth says simply, looking straight towards me.

"We have shared blood before and have a bond, he can have mine," I reply, knowing that I don't care about sharing blood with Korbin. Even if we weren't bonded already, I would still happily give him my blood.

"It will make you weak, and with the amount of blood he will need, it will create a permanent bond," Darth warns me, and my eyes flash to Elias, who simply nods. I know he will support me no matter what I choose. I look down at Korbin and squeeze his hand tighter.

"I know you're not awake to make this decision, but I will save you," I tell him and look up to Darth who is watching us with a sad smile.

"We are permanent, anyway. I will *not* lose him," I say, keeping my eyes locked on Darth's, and he nods, a small smile on his lips.

"Let's get you all set up in the other room then. I will take as much blood as I can without hurting you, every two hours. Our dragons speed up blood loss, and that should be okay for Korbin. This isn't a fix for the poison, but it will give me time to examine and figure out what he needs to heal him," Darth explains to me and Elias.

"Take what you need," I reply.

"Your dragon needs to be okay with this, is she?" Darth enquires, "I don't want an angry dragon bursting out in my room and freezing me."

"Save minnnee," my dragon hisses in response, and I watch Darth almost smile as he sees my eyes change.

"She will do anything to save him. We have always been in agreement about my guards," I reply, and I feel Elias gently stroke my arm with his fingers.

"Right then, let's get started," Darth says, picking up a bundle of things from a box and walking out of the room. I move closer to Korbin, leaning down and kissing his sweaty, boiling hot forehead and hearing him mumble my name.

"I'm here. I'm always here for you, Kor," I tell him gently, seeing him slowly relax and his breathing even out before I straighten up. I don't want to leave him, but I know I have to. Elias waits for me by the door, holding it open with his back. I slip past him, and he stops me, grabbing my hip with his one hand and using the other to place a finger under my chin, making me look up into his swirling blue eyes. I raise my hand, moving a stray piece of black hair out of his eyes and trailing my finger down his face as he carefully watches me.

"He will survive this, for you. Don't look so scared, I hate seeing it in your eyes," Elias admits in a whisper.

"I've never felt like this, not for anyone until I met you three. I thought losing Jace devastated me, but I know if I lose any of you, I would be completely ruined," I say gently, placing my hand on Elias's chest. He closes his eyes, leaning forward to rest his forehead against mine. The little contact soothes me, reminds me that I have them and that they are not going anywhere.

"Neither have I ever felt like I do for you, and it scares the fuck out of me, princess. You know, I thought I was brave and fearless, but I'm *nothing* compared to you. You make me so proud with how brave you are. You are my inspiration to keep fighting, to push through, even though I've fought my whole life for nothing but survival," he whispers, as

I watch him so closely, taking in every part of his complexion, his handsome features as he makes my heart flutter in my chest.

"Eli," I sigh, my emotions leaking out into that one word, and he moves a tiny inch closer as he opens his eyes.

"Excuse me. Now, I don't need to see you two kissing when I have things I need to be doing, like saving your friend's life," Darth's slightly amused voice comes over to us, and Elias backs away, letting me pass through the door. Darth is standing in the open doorway of the room opposite, and nods his head towards me, inviting me in.

"I'm going to keep an eye out downstairs," Elias tells me as I look back at him, seeing desire and longing swirling in his eyes but knowing there isn't anything we can do about it right now. Something always seems to come between us, every time we start to get close. It's like fate is finding it fun to keep us apart, with only brushes of stolen kisses to keep us going. Elias turns, walking down the stairs as I go into the small bedroom where Darth is waiting for me. There isn't much in here, but it's cosy. There is a double bed, with torn blue sheets covering it and matching blue curtains on the window. In the window is a vase of flowers, but they are all dead and look like they have been there for years.

"Sit on the bed, girl," Darth says distractedly as he looks through his box that he has placed on the floor. I watch him searching through the box, taking things out and putting others back, so focused on the job at hand, and all I can think about is how he knew my mother once. There aren't that many people alive who knew her and a deep part of me wants to know as much as I can about her. I guess I could ask about my father at the same time, but I don't. Every time I think about him, I just remember Melody. How my father betrayed my mother, had a child with another woman, and couldn't even man up enough to tell me about her.

"What was my mother like? If you don't mind me asking. It's only, I don't remember much, and there is no one alive to tell me more things about her," I ask.

"Tatarina is alive and knew your mother more than anyone, well, before she married your father at least. After the marriage, they never spoke because of your father," he says, with a slight chuckle as he carries a handful of things over to the bed, placing them next to me and sitting next to them. "Take your cloak off and pull your right arm sleeve up." I do what he asks and place the cloak on the pillow. Darth taps the inside of my arm a few times before sliding a needle inside and taping it down. The needle has a long tube connected to it, that goes into a jar.

"Are all these clean?" I ask, seeing that the jar isn't a great colour and doubt the needle is.

"Clean as we can get when we are poor and not in the castle. Your dragon blood will keep you alive, do not worry. You aren't human after all," he says, watching my blood pour into the jar. I decide to leave it for now. It doesn't much matter, like he said, and I have to stop thinking like a human. I remember his comment about Tatarina and decide to answer it.

"Tatarina would sooner kill me than tell me anything about my mother. Not that I could trust a word she speaks, anyway," I say, still not fully processing the fact that mine and Thorne's mothers were so close.

"There isn't much to tell, not much you do not already know. Vivian was kind and gentle . . . and honestly, not built to be a queen. She couldn't make the hard decisions, and a simple life would have been better for her, but she was oh, so beautiful. No man could resist her, much like her daughter seems to have caught the hearts of many also," he says, not looking at me as he stares out of the window, lost in his thoughts and likely his memories. I instantly feel jealous that I can't see his memories of my mother.

"Do you think someone kind and gentle shouldn't have the throne?" I ask.

"No, someone who is brave, selfless, strict, and kind should have the throne. They would be best to make the decisions they will face. Yet, we cannot get all those things in one person," he muses.

"I have to take the throne back from Tatarina," I whisper into the now silent room.

"Yes, but it will not be easy. Tatarina was one of the selected before she became queen, and her son later killed the king." I go to correct him, that Tatarina killed my father, but decide not to as I don't want to interrupt him. "She has always been in power and knows Dragca better than anyone else. Well, perhaps not as well as her son, but he is not strong enough to rule and kill his mother." I don't directly reply, but when he looks over at me, I know he feels my agreement to his statement in my eyes. Thorne is smart, but he cares too much for his mother to do what is right in the end. He is blinded when it comes to her, and I'm anxious about telling him what I know of his mother, worried he won't believe me.

"Why is she like this?" I have to ask, because I want to understand what happened to make her so cruel. She sent someone to kill my mother, a childhood friend, and then she mated to the husband left behind. Only someone truly evil could do something like that. Only someone with no soul.

"Some say a dark spirit came to her on the day of the royal mating between your father and mother. Her jealousy, hate, and anger called out to the dark spirit, and since then her heart has been darkened. I truly believe it. I saw Tatarina a few years back, and even her appearance is darker than it's ever been. Her blonde hair is a mustard colour, and her light-blue eyes are now a dark-blue."

"So, the dark spirit, the darkness has changed her?" I ask.

"Yes, and I believe when you start using your light powers, you will change, too," he says, and I wonder if he is right. I guess I will know soon, when I finally get the time to start using the light. I may be scared of its unpredictability, but I'm not stupid enough not to recognize that I can't beat Tatarina without it.

"Can any part of her be saved?" I ask, thinking

only of Thorne. She is still his mother, and I know what it's like to lose one. Thorne has already lost his birth father, his adoptive parents, and his aunt. Even if most of them deserved their deaths, he doesn't deserve to lose another relative if it can be avoided.

"He is better off without her alive. The world is. Child, I know little of light and dark spirits, but where there is one, there must be another," he smiles, looking down at the jar that is half full.

"The darkness must be destroyed," I whisper, and he flashes me a sad smile.

"You cannot destroy something that has existed before Dragca, before life, before even time, itself. Darkness and light are equally needed and equally cursed by one another," he tells me, but still seems sad to do so. I don't reply as I look out the window he was looking out of, seeing the two suns high in the sky and how bright they look. Sun comes before the night, and light comes with darkness. *God, my life is starting to sound like a movie, and I won't be surprised if something else goes wrong at this point.*

"How is Korbin doing?" I ask groggily, lifting my head from the pillow as Melody steps into the room with a small tray full of food. I rub my arm as Bee flies out of her bag, coming over to me and landing on my hip. She sits down as Melody puts the food on the dresser. I'm not really hungry because the blood loss is making me feel sick, but I will try to eat later.

"Dagan is with him, and he still hasn't woken. The healer is doing his best," she answers, but not really answering the question I asked. I want to know if he is doing better, if he looks better, or anything other than the fact he hasn't woken up yet. It's been a day since we got here, and I've done countless blood exchanges. I lie back on the pillow, feeling Bee stroking my arm as I look at my sister. She doesn't have her cloak on now, and her black hair is down, covering her serious expression as she opens her bag. The look on her face somewhat reminds me of my father. Well, *our* father. Something I don't know how to get used to.

"Did Thorne come back?" I ask.

"He is back, and not speaking to anyone. He just spent the last half an hour cleaning the kitchen," she tells me.

"I didn't know he cleaned," I say aimlessly.

"Tired?" Bee asks me, distracting me from my thoughts as she slides off me and chooses to lie on the bed right next to me instead.

"Yeah, a little. Are you okay?" I ask her, and she nods, curling up in a little ball.

"We need light . . . soon . . . darkness is rising," she mumbles, yawning loudly before falling to sleep. *Nothing like some cryptic, scary words from a spirit to make you feel better.* I pull the blanket up, covering her body before looking over at Melody who holds her orb. I'd seen them at a distance when I was a kid, but I never really understood them or what connection they have to seers. Most seers have their orbs on a sceptre, which I remember seeing many seers walking around with them like a walking stick.

Suddenly, I remember Melody's mother as a flash-back flitters into my mind.

"Princess, you should not be out here alone," a warm, kind voice says from just behind me, and I spin around, looking up at the royal seer. She has long black hair, brown eyes, and black swirls on her face that look like someone drew on her.

"I had to put the bird outside, it flew into my room," I explain, holding the little bird up to show her, and she smiles.

"That is very kind of you, but you should still have guards with you. You are the princess, and so very important to Dragca. Let's put the bird down and find your personal guards," she says, holding out a hand. I put the bird down on the floor, watching as it hops a little before flying away. I accept the seer's hand, smiling up at her as we walk back through the gardens.

"Your name isn't seer, is it?" I ask, curious.

"No, why do you think that?" she replies.

"Everyone calls you 'seer', or 'royal seer'. It's confusing," I say, gigging a little, and it makes her laugh.

"My name is Savannah."

· · ·

THE MEMORY LEAVES my mind as I look back over to Melody, who is staring into her orb. Her eyes glow a warm bright blue, and she carefully places her hand on the orb as sadness washes over her face. She looks so much like her mother. They have the same features, and the same mysterious air seems to surround her, just like it did her mother. Everything good about her seems to have come from her mother, and luckily, she only seems to have my father's eyes. I'm starting to believe my father was never the good guy in any situation. Maybe everyone isn't good or bad though, and my father had good parts in him.

"Bee tried to help Darth heal Korbin, but it didn't work. Bee said the poison is from the dark, and that it is immune to light," Melody tells me, and I frown. How are we going to stop it from killing Korbin, then?

"What did Darth say when he saw her?" I ask, stroking Bee's green hair. It's so soft, fine, and full of glitter.

"He wasn't that shocked. He said he once saw Tatarina's dark spirit, and a light one isn't all that different," she says, and goes back to focusing on the orb. I guess that makes sense. I wonder what makes dark and light spirits look different? I'm curious to find out, but at the same time, I don't want to have to fight the dark.

"What do orbs do?" I ask, snapping her out of the connection she has going with the orb, and she looks up, not bothering to hide the sad look.

"Boosts our natural powers, allows us to see people, but we have to have a connection to who we want to see. It's how I could watch you when you were on earth," Melody explains and stands up, walking over to me. She climbs onto the bed on my other side, and I pull myself up, careful not to wake Bee. I sit with my back against the headboard, with Melody snuggled in right next to me.

"Who were you looking at just now?" I ask gently.

"Hallie," she whispers, confusing me.

"I thought you needed a connection? I didn't know you and Hallie were connected by anything other than fake memories," I say. Melody places her hand on the side of the orb, her eyes glow as smoke fills the inside of the orb, swirling around and around before an image comes into view. The image starts off blurry, then fills out. Hallie is sitting at a desk in what looks like an office. There isn't much in the room, just a grey desk, filing cabinets, and I can see a door behind her. Hallie isn't moving, just staring at the wall, tapping her fingers on the desk. Her hair is dyed purple at the tips, not the blue it was when I last saw her, and she has glasses on, no contacts, which instantly worries me. Hallie hates to wear her glasses.

"Her father has had her locked in this room for the last two weeks. No bed. Little food, and plenty of interrogation from both him and the people that work with him," Melody says, her voice cracking ever so slightly.

"What?" I ask in alarm, looking back down at Hallie. She looks normal like she usually does, though maybe a little paler and tired. The door opens, and a man I don't know walks in, just as smoke fills the orb, and the image disappears.

"Wait, who was that?" I ask Melody. "Actually, that doesn't matter, we need to rescue her from her father!" Melody gently places her hand on my shoulder, stopping me from trying to get up even when how weak I feel stops me anyway.

"If I could do anything to help her, I would have already. There is nothing you can do, and he won't kill her. That's all that matters," she says, but her excuse seems weak. She wants to help, but I don't get why she is so emotional about this.

"Who is Hallie to you?" I ask quietly.

"I told you that I saw my future girlfriend once?" she asks, and it clicks into place as I remember Melody mentioned that she never sees herself in visions, except for one of her and her future girlfriend.

"Hallie is your future girlfriend?" I ask.

"Yep. Sucks that she isn't into girls right now, or at least, she hasn't admitted it to herself. With everything that will happen, I don't know if we will ever have a future like I saw," she says, and wipes one shaky hand across her cheek. It must be horrible to watch someone you know is destined for you with other people and now being hurt.

"You will," I grab her hand on the orb, and it burns where my fingers graze the orb, making me sharply pull my hand away. I look down at my hand and see little burn marks. Fire doesn't burn me . . . but the orb can?

"Crap, sorry. I didn't expect you to touch it. Orbs burn any dragon. They can't be touched by your kind," she explains, moving the orb away a little like she is worried I would be crazy enough to try and touch it again.

"I've never been burnt before," I whisper, kind of amazed.

"I forget you don't know much about Dragca . . .

most dragons know not to touch orbs," she chuckles which makes me smile.

"Where did you get your orb from?" I ask.

"It was my mother's. Orbs are passed down within families, well, usually. If the family has no heirs for the orb, it is returned to where all orbs come from," she says.

"Where?" I ask.

"No one knows. I've heard they just disappear," she replies, shrugging her shoulders and making her black hair fall over them.

"That's sad," I comment.

"I thought I wouldn't be able to touch the orb, being half dragon, but, apparently, my dragon side didn't stop my inheritance," she states. I bet she was nervous to try and touch it the first time.

"Do you hear your dragon in your mind?" I ask her, curious. I can't smell dragon on her, not like you would expect. I can only smell her seer side, so her dragon side must be well hidden.

"No. I've never had that, or any powers from my ice dragon side, except one," she smiles, looking at my hand. "I can't be burnt either."

"That's a good power to receive," I say.

"Can I give you some advice? As your loving

sister, as well as someone that wants you back on the throne," she asks, and I nod.

"I wouldn't flaunt your relationships with your dragon guards. If you want the seers to side with you, and if you want the dragons to, you can't be seen to be in love with dragon guards who have no dragons. You can't be seen to publicly choose them over the throne. They are a weakness to you now, one that can and will be used against you by your enemies. Don't let everyone see what they mean to you, don't wear your emotions on your face quite so much," she advises me.

"I don't want to hide how I feel, it's not going to change anything, and I *would* choose them over the throne. If they can't accept my dragon guards as my–" I go to say 'mates' when I realise they have never asked me to mate with them.

"Mates. They will be your mates, I don't need a vision to know that's what you want from those smoking hot dragons, sis," she teases, and I laugh.

"It's all still so new to us, and everything is going wrong. It's not the right time to be planning long-term stuff when none of us knows what our future will hold," I say.

"What do you *want* for your future?"

"I guess I don't really think that far ahead

anymore. Everything has become a fight for each day, and it never leaves me time to dream of an ending to this. I guess I only want the dragon guards' curse to be broken, for Kor to live, and for me to kill Tatarina. Those are my main concerns for now," I tell her.

"The seers might know how to break the curse, or at least they might have an idea."

"Really? I could get back their dragons?"

"Maybe, but you need the seers to side with you first. You need them to believe you are the rightful queen, and one who will always put Dragca first before *anything* else," she firmly tells me. I know she has a point, yet I don't want the seers' decision to side with me based on lies. I don't want the throne if deceit and half-truths are the only way to overthrow Tatarina and secure the crown.

"How do you feel about Thorne now?" Melody enquires, trying to sound innocent, but the tiny smirk on her lips gives her away.

"He betrayed me, and then he saved me. I guess I don't know. Thorne has always had the uncanny ability to confuse me, even from the very first time we met. It's strange, because even when he is pushing me away, betraying me, and downright being an idiot, I still want to be near him. I know I could never hurt him, and what's worse is that I understand *why* he did everything he did. I don't forgive him yet, but I do understand most of it," I admit, and she takes my hand, leaving the orb in her lap.

"Love doesn't care about circumstances. It just turns up, wrecks your life, and somehow has the ability to make you the happiest you can ever be," she says.

"My sister is pretty smart, huh?" I gently bump her shoulder, and she laughs.

"About time you noticed," she says with a grin and rests her head on my shoulder.

"When we don't have all this stuff going on, and our lives are kind of sorted . . . I want to get to know you, find out more about your life. We missed out on a childhood together, but we can make up for that," I comment.

"Deal," she whispers.

"Pinky promise?" I ask, holding out my pinky finger and wiggling it, and she frowns at me like I've lost my mind. Whoops, I forgot seers wouldn't know about human things.

"What is that?" she asks slowly.

"Something humans do on Earth that means you promise never to break the promise. I know it's silly, but there were these siblings I grew up at human school with. They always pinky promised things, and I used to be jealous I never had a sister or brother to do that with," I explain to her. Jace wouldn't do it with me, because he didn't like things that humans came up with and said the idea was stupid. Melody links her pinky finger with mine.

"I pinky promise," she says, and all I can do is grin.

SEVEN

ISOLA

"You should be resting, girl. It's the middle of the night," Darth chides as I step into Korbin's room, and I softly close the door behind me. Darth is sitting on a chair next to Korbin's bed, but I barely even register his presence. Korbin is sitting up on the bed, his green eyes watching me as his lips tilt up with a little smile.

"She was never good at doing what she was told," Korbin teases, his voice croaky as I run over to him and wrap my arms around his chest.

"You're awake," I say, pulling back, and he smiles widely, looking as happy as I feel at seeing him awake. Korbin still has purple lines crawling up his face, close to his eyes, and he looks extremely pale, but he is awake, and that's an improvement. Any improvement seems like a blessing right now.

"I'm tired, but trying to stay awake for a bit," he says groggily, and I kiss him lightly before sitting back. I hold onto his hand as I look over at Darth.

"Is he going to be okay now?" I ask, and Darth shakes his head.

"A temporary fix. I don't have the magic, or the right medicine to heal him, and I have no advice on where you can find it," Darth admits and looks at Korbin. "Your parents . . . they might be able to help, or at least pay for the right kind of help."

"They will be with the seers, and we are going that way anyway," Korbin says.

"Then I will come with you to keep you alive. We will leave in the morning," Darth states, standing up slowly.

"Why are you so willing to help me?" Korbin asks.

"Your parents, I knew them very well. We had a falling out many, many years ago. Let's just say I owe them, and keeping their only son alive is a good start at repayment," Darth explains and then leaves the room as we silently watch him go. I look back up at Korbin, just running my eyes over him to check he is okay. Just needing to see that he is, at least for now.

"Lie with me? I just want to hold you for a bit," Korbin asks, and I do, resting my head on his chest.

"Dagan and Elias told me about what my father said to you. They said my father trusted your parents," I whisper, yet my voice still feels like it carries around the room.

"I wanted to tell you sooner. Every morning, running with you, and keeping a secret from you, it wasn't easy because I fell for you the moment we met. I knew your father was right, that the prophecy was right, as soon as I met you, and I wanted you safe from that moment on," he slowly tells me.

"I felt something from the very start, too. I did with you all, but I tried to play it off because I was grieving over Jace," I voice something I haven't even wanted to admit to myself. It feels like I betrayed Jace by just feeling it, much less saying it out loud.

"I'm sorry Jace died, I have a feeling I would have liked him. You know, after we fought over you and agreed we could both love you at the same time," he jokes, and I sigh.

"Jace would have kicked all your asses," I mutter, but I'm not actually sure who would have won.

"I don't doubt he would have tried. I wouldn't

want to share you, not if I met you first and had you to myself for so long," he muses.

"Are you okay with everything? The fact that I want to be with Elias and Dagan, too?" I ask quietly after a comfortable silence between us.

"At first, no. I couldn't swallow the thought of sharing you and having you love someone else. I was scared you would love them more than me," he tells me, his hand holding mine tightly.

"That won't happen," I say, looking up at him, and he stares up at the ceiling.

"Then I realised something. You loved them anyway, had the whole time we were together, and you still loved me the same. Loving more than one person doesn't make you love less, it just makes you love more," he says, his words making me smile like a crazy person because they are so sweet. And so true.

"Such a romantic. If you weren't ill, then I'd be swooning and doing sexy things to you," I say, making him laugh.

"I'll hold you to that offer when I'm better, doll," he whispers. "Thank you for saving me, giving me all that blood when you knew it would make our bond stronger. We never did have a second to talk about that."

"You did it for me once, how could I not do the same for you?" I reply.

"One day, when we have a moment to ourselves . . . would you mate with me?" he asks suddenly, casually like he didn't just ask something very important and life changing. I sharply sit up, leaning over him. My hair falls like a curtain around us as I stare down at him.

"Really? You want me? Forever?" I ask, completely in shock. *He must still be ill.*

"You have me forever, even if we don't mate. I don't care what I am to you, mate, lover, friend, or even ex-lover. I just want to be with you," he says, and I go to answer him when the door bursts open behind us. I jerk up to see Elias running in.

"The guards are searching the houses. They know we are here, we have to go!" Elias shouts, panicked, and runs over to help me get Korbin up as I slide off him. Korbin holds an arm around my shoulder, and the other on Elias as we hurry out of the room and down the stairs.

"Isola needs to fly everyone out, it's the only way," I hear Darth demand as we get to the bottom of the stairs.

"She can't fly us all, and the barrier . . ." Thorne

shakes his head as he watches out the window, not looking back at us once as he speaks.

"I *can* fly all of you, at least far enough to make it out of the town. I'll land in the forest, and we can run and hide," I say, sending the thought to my dragon. I know she is bigger than most dragons and strong. Let's hope strong enough as I'm not leaving anyone behind to deal with the guards.

"*Yes, but not far. Tired,*" she replies, sending worry crashing into my head.

"I can drop the barrier for a second, I just need my orb to touch it. It will knock me out though, as it's a lot of magic," Melody explains. "It will also let the seer who made the barrier know where we are. They might look for us, which would be a good thing."

"We will protect you after you destroy the barrier," Dagan tells her, and I nod at her in confirmation.

"They are two doors away," Thorne says, shutting the curtain quickly and stepping away.

"We go into the garden, and Isola you need to shift quickly. Everyone ready?" Darth commands us all, picking up a bag and walking to the fireplace. He picks up a small picture frame, kissing it once before sliding it into his bag.

"Sorry about this, man, but we need a quick

escape," Elias says, picking Korbin up by the waist and flinging him over his shoulder. "What the hell do you eat, you weigh a ton," Elias groans.

"Asshole," Korbin groggily replies as we walk to the back door. I go to step out when a hand stops me, and I look up to see it's Thorne.

"Let me go first, we don't know if anyone is out there," he commands, like I should listen to his every word.

"That's why I should go first," I mutter, glaring at his back as he gently pushes past me and out of the door. I don't wait as I follow him out, seeing a stone garden filled with stone ornaments of dragons, wings, and various other beautiful things. They all look handmade, and clearly someone put a lot of effort into making this garden as beautiful as it is.

"I'm going to break everything by shifting out here," I say to no one in particular.

"I'd rather you break my wife's statues than the guards break us. Get on with the shift, girl!" Darth barks out, and I nod sadly at him. I walk straight into the middle of the garden and close my eyes, letting my dragon take over. When I open my eyes, everything is sharper, and I look over to see everyone standing at the door. My dragon lowers herself down, crushing the statues as she does, and even my dragon seems to realise. Elias climbs up my wing first, followed by Dagan, Melody, Darth, and Thorne last.

"Over here!" I hear someone shout. My sensitive ears pick up the sound from what could be a good distance away, but regardless, they know we are here, and we can't fight them like this.

"Fly straight up, close enough for Melody to touch the barrier, but don't let yourself touch it. I don't want you hurt," I say to my dragon, and she bats her wings out, flying up in the air and knocking a stone wall over on her way up.

"Shoot her! Don't let her fly away!" I hear a guard scream, and then dozens of arrows fly at us, hitting our right wing and making my dragon roar. She turns around, mid-flight.

"Freeze," I hear her hiss, and I don't disagree as she shoots a blast of ice at the guards, freezing them all on the spot while they try to reload their arrows. Two guards manage to escape, and I see them shifting moments before they fly up into the air, breathing out fire.

"Get to the barrier! We can't fight them with the others on our backs!" I try to reason with her, and thankfully, she does as I ask, speeding away even when her wing hurts from the arrows that fall away

in the wind. She gets close to the barrier, gliding in the air as streams of fire hit our tail from the dragons following us. My dragon turns her head back in time to see Melody place her orb against the barrier, holding it firmly in place as the orb flashes brightly. A white light blasts out, blinding us all for a moment, and then the barrier falls away in little blue sparks.

"Fly away! Now!" I plead with my dragon, and she flies off, straight into the woods. I hear her cry reverberate in my ears as the forest gets a little blurry, and the surrounding sounds seem to buzz against our ears. I know her wing is hurt, and she can't last long, but those dragons must still be following us. The last thing I'm aware of before darkness claims me is my dragon plummeting, crashing into the forest, and the screams of our passengers as she falls.

EIGHT

DAGAN

I brush the dirt and hair out of my face, jumping up off the ground as everything swirls for a moment, and I try to focus on what happened. Isola was flying one second, and then crashing the next. Something had to be wrong for her to fall like that. Thank god, we weren't too high when she turned on her side and dropped us in the trees. I quickly scan my surroundings, knowing I need to find her and seeing no one else near me.

"Isola!" I shout, and no one replies. Shit. A guard steps out from behind a tree, holding a sword, and smirking when he sees me. I quickly pull out my own sword, holding it at my side as I examine the guard. He is young and fairly small. I doubt he is trained well from the way he rushed out here rather than planning out his attack.

"Bring it on," I say, wanting to get this out of the way. He rushes at me, lifting his sword behind his neck and slamming it down on mine, and I elbow his face when he lets his guard down for a second. I kick his stomach as he drops his sword in shock and falls on the floor. I pick up his sword, walking over and holding it against his neck.

"Don't shift, don't move. Now, you can run away and deal with the queen hunting you, or you die by my hand now," I warn.

"I-I had no choice. The queen made my father join the dragon guard. She said she would kill my mother if he didn't. I have four brothers, and we all got cursed with him," he replies.

"I am truly sorry for that, but make your choice," I honestly tell him.

"I will run," he says dejectedly, his voice an echo as I watch his whole body glow red for a second, and then I see the pain in his eyes. His dragon knows the queen knows he has betrayed her. She will send guards to hunt him now. The curse always makes sure the ruler knows when they have been betrayed. Which means I need him to run and get as far away from Isola and me as possible.

"Run and don't stop running," I say, moving my sword away, and he runs into the forest, never looking back once.

"Watch out!" I hear Melody shout, and I look up just in time to see her jump down. I quickly move out the way as I put my sword back in its sheath and throw the other in a nearby bush.

"You okay?" I ask her, and she shakily nods. Bee flies down to us, following Melody.

"Isola?" Bee asks, searching for her in the trees and frowning.

"Bee, can you fly up and see if you can find anyone? If you notice any other dragons, don't let them see you," Melody asks her, and she nods, flying up the tree.

"Isola was hurt, we need to find her," I state.

"Agreed. We need to find the others and get out of here. The guards will be searching for us," Melody tells me what I already know. Thankfully, at least one of them isn't searching for us, and there were only two that shifted and followed us. That only leaves one guard, and I'm hopeful he won't find us. We wait silently until Bee flies down, sitting on Melody's shoulder.

"That way," Bee points to our left, where we can

see nothing but more trees, and we have no choice but to trust her.

"Keep your eyes open," I tell Melody, who nods, sliding a dagger out her pocket as I pull my sword out. We carefully step through the trees, our feet crunching on branches with every step, and I'm way too aware of how loud we are being. Any guards would be able to hear us with their sensitive hearing from their dragons. We trudge through the forest until we come to a clearing of smashed trees that leads to a little cliff, and I know Isola must have crashed here and skidded all the way down. I run out of the clearing, only seeing more trees at the bottom of the cliff.

"Damn, we will have to climb down," I say, rubbing my jaw.

"Dagan!" I hear my name shouted, and I turn, freezing at the sight of a man I don't know holding Isola in his arms. She is unconscious, her head hangs from one of his arms, but she doesn't look dead, though blood drips down her right arm. It doesn't look good, not with the three arrow marks I can see from here. The man keeps his eyes on me, and I see that he is massive, with dark-red hair and red tattoos littered down his arms. I breathe a sigh of relief that she is alive, and step forward, only pausing when Melody stops me.

"Give her to us," I demand.

"No," the man says simply, a large grin spreading across his face as he looks down at Isola. *The fucker.*

"Enough. We didn't come here to discuss anything, and we cannot stay long," a woman says, stepping out of the shadows of the trees. About twenty other people follow out after her, all covered in weapons, and they aren't dragon guards. I keep my eyes on the woman that spoke. The way she stands slightly in front of them all tells me all I need to know; she is the leader here. The woman has long black hair, tanned skin, and most of her face is hidden in her cloak. She lowers her cloak, showing me her black eyes and the black marks on her face.

Seer.

"Let the princess go," I command, and she laughs.

"You have no authority here, Dagan Fire. Do not push me," the woman says, and I let out a loud growl, my eyes never leaving Isola in that idiot's hands. I'm going to kill him for touching her.

"We were looking for you," Melody says, stepping in front of me with Bee on her shoulder. The woman's eyes go straight to Bee, as do every other seer's and dragon's here. I've gotten used to seeing her, but for most, it is still a shock.

"It's true. The light has returned," the woman says, breathing out her words slowly like she can't believe them.

"Do you support the dark?" Melody asks, and there is complete silence except for a few gasps of shock.

"No." The one word answer comes from the woman, and she steps closer.

"We request safe travel, for all of us, and for you to give Isola a chance. My mother was your last leader, and Isola is my sister. Will you refuse me?" Melody asks, holding her head high as she glares at the woman. If Melody's mother was the last leader, surely Melody should be the one leading them now?

"You side with the lost princess?" the woman asks, almost laughing.

"The princess is the one that *should* be queen, as she is who the light has chosen. Not everything is clear, but unless you plan to kill the last light today . . . you will help us," Melody states.

"My name is Essna, the current leader of the seers, and I accept your request. We will take you all back, as prisoners, and wait for the princess to wake up. She may yet be the queen we need," Essna says, and Melody bows, stepping back to my side as I rush past her.

"Let me hold the princess, and we need to find the others before we leave," I say, seeing the smirk on the asshole's lips as he holds her close to his chest. I'm going to knock that smile off his lips the first chance I get.

"No. She needs a healer, and yours is currently unconscious from the fall. We have taken the other dragon guards. The one is very ill, and the other put up a good fight. You will behave, or I will put you in the prison until you control your emotions," Essna says.

"I'm sorry for this, but I know your stubborn ass will fight them," Melody says from my l left as she quickly places her hand on my head, sending blinding white light flashing through my mind.

CHAPTER
NINE
ISOLA

*I*sola. Isola. Make the deal, make the trade. Light *must win, and darkness cannot fade. Make the deal, make the trade, but remember that balance must be gained . . . .*

I groan as I wake up, hearing the echo of a female voice singing the song like a whisper in my ear, but when I open my eyes, the unfamiliar room is empty, and I'm just left feeling cold. I flinch when I try to use my arm to sit up, and I look down to see the white bandage covering my entire arm, stopping at my wrist and at the top of my shoulder. It's spotted with my blood, but it's not too painful. I frown as I realise I have no clothes on, terror filling me until I feel like I can't breathe. I pull the brown sheets tighter around me, moving back on the bed and closing my eyes, trying to calm down.

I'm not on Earth. Michael is dead. I need to relax. I repeat the same words, time and time again until I can think a little more clearly. It comes back to me that I shifted and lost my clothes, but it doesn't stop the panic from rising again that anyone could have found me naked in the forest. *Dagan. Elias. Korbin. Thorne. Home.* Repeating those words in my head instead of thinking of anything else helps me breathe, helps me calm down. When I can finally open my eyes, I see I've frozen most of the sheet and the straw walls of the hut I'm in. *Hut?* I look around, seeing it's a basic circle hut made out of straw that is tied at the top. A small firepit in the middle of the hut, the bed I'm on, and a dresser next to a fabric door are the only furnishings.

"What happened?" I ask my dragon, but say it out loud, figuring she'll be listening.

We fell. I do not know more. We must find mine, she hisses, and I feel her frustration and worry ramping up and blending with my own. She thinks she hurt them, and she knows my arm is not going to heal for a while, so I can't shift. I'm torn from examining my dragon's emotions when the fabric door is pushed aside, and a woman walks in. The woman is wearing a brown cloak tied in the middle with a belt. Her brown hair is up in a bun, and she doesn't look my way as she closes the fabric door behind her.

"Who are you?" I ask firmly, sliding off the bed and standing tall, even as I hold my blanket up with one hand. The woman bows her head, and her scent hits me. *Human.* "Am I on Earth?" The woman doesn't answer my question, walking over to the dresser and opening the drawers. She pulls out a bundle of leather clothes and a cloak before coming over to me.

"My name is Jenny. I am human, but you are not on Earth. I fell into Dragca twenty years ago after running away from my family. I serve the seers, and in return, the seers keep me alive. I was sent to help you get dressed, as our leader wishes to meet you," she says and finally looks up at me, her harsh eyes meeting mine.

"Where are my dragon guards? My sister?" I demand.

"I cannot give you the answers you want, but I can only suggest that letting me help you get dressed and meeting our leader might get you the answers you need, princess," she answers, but her voice is still hard and cold. There is nothing warm about her, and I wonder if that's why she was sent to me, because she can't be swayed.

"Fine," I mutter, moving aside, so she can place the clothes on the bed.

"I will be over here if you need help. Your arm should not be moved much. The healer said you would need help getting dressed," she says.

"I don't need help, but thank you," I reply, because one way or the other, I'm getting myself dressed on my own. Jenny sharply looks away and walks over to the dresser, facing the wall. I drop the blanket, picking up the leather tank top and sliding it over one arm, before carefully putting my injured arm though the hole. I bite my lip as I pull the tight tank top down over my head and down my body. It stops just under my boobs, holding them up like a sports bra instead of a shirt because it's so tight. They must have been made for someone a lot smaller. I sit down on the bed, pulling the tight leather trousers on, that resemble three quarter lengths by the time I get them up and then click the cloak around my neck.

"Let me sort that hair of yours out. No princess should see anyone with that rat's nest of hair. I washed your hair when you were sleeping, and washed you down, if you wondered why you are clean. You smelt bad, and I found more dirt in your hair than actual hair," Jenny says in disgust, but it makes me laugh in relief that it was her that looked after me and no one else. I look up to see her holding a chair out with a hairbrush in her hand. I smile, walking over, and sitting down.

"Thank you," I say, and flinch as she roughly brushes my hair. I guess it was messy. It takes twenty minutes for her to brush it all, and she plaits the top of my hair, so it falls into a long plait down my back in the middle of the waves of blonde curly hair.

"Now, that's much better," Jenny claps, and I stand up, my long hair falling to my waist, and smooth down my cloak. "There is a mirror over there." I follow Jenny's pointed finger to where there is a full-length mirror hanging on the wall. I stare at myself for a second, noting how much older and worried I look. I don't look confident. I look scared, and my blue eyes seem to show my every emotion. Melody is right. I need to hide my emotions better if I want to make it through this. I steel my gaze, lift my head up, and straighten my back. I am Isola Dragice. This is my world, and I will not be a frightened little girl anymore.

I'm blinded by the sunlight for only a moment as I step outside the hut and smell the scents of multiple dragons and seers, all of them unfamiliar. There are five huts on each side of a white stone path that has lanterns on wood sticks following along each side. Jenny walks down the path, and I follow just behind her, glancing around, taking stock of my surroundings to get an idea of where I am. There isn't much to see, other than woods and the sun shining high in the sky. We could be in any forest, and unfortunately, Dragca is full of them. I don't have any more time to look as I notice Jenny is nearly out of my sight, and I jog to catch up with her. The path winds around more huts until I can see a massive crowd of people gathered around something.

The people turn one by one to stare at me, some lowering their heads in respect, but many just stare blankly. I spot some seers, some dragons, and even catch the scents of a few humans in the crowd. As we get to the people, they part to make a small path through them, but I feel the eyes of so many of them on me, judging me. I keep my eyes forward and my head high as we walk into the clearing. I see a woman sitting on a wooden chair, one that almost resembles a throne. She has long black hair, seer marks on her forehead that are similar to Melody's, and a very serious expression. Next to her, are two sets of seers in cloaks, each holding long sceptres with orbs on top in front of them. I skim the crowd, searching for any of my dragon guards or my sister, but not seeing them.

"They are here and on their way, princess," the seer woman says, like she knows my thoughts.

"Good. Are they well?" I ask, continuing forward and leaving Jenny in the crowd. I stop right in front of the woman, and she stands up, towering over me as she is much taller. I still keep eye contact and hold my ground.

"Is that really the only question you wish to ask,

lost princess?" she chuckles and starts walking around me with measured steps, examining me slowly. "Don't you want to ask if you are a prisoner about to meet her death . . . or if we side with you?"

"I will not ask either of those because I already know the answer. Yes, I am your prisoner, and you do not know whether you want to side with me or not. If you didn't want to truly consider which queen you want on the throne, I would be dead already," I reply, and she nods, going back to her seat and sitting down. We watch each other closely, neither one of us saying a word as the warm wind blows my hair around my face.

"Isola!" I hear Dagan shout, and I turn, seeing him, Elias, and Thorne being dragged through the crowd in handcuffs. They all look a bit worse for wear, especially Elias, who is covered in dirt and has a cut on his cheek. I go to step towards them when Melody walks out of the crowd, shaking her head as she stops next to Elias. She isn't handcuffed, and she has clean clothes on. A light-blue cloak, leather clothes, and she has clearly showered. So, they apparently trust her.

"The princess that is always lost wants us to fight for her!" the woman shouts out, catching my attention, and there is laughter in the crowd as my cheeks light up.

"Essna, you must hear her out," Melody shouts back, pushing past a seer that tries to stop her and comes to stand at my side.

"I have listened to you all day, and I understand what you need . . . but I know from one look where her loyalty lies. What the princess *truly* wants," Essna says, her blue eyes watching me like she has won some great prize.

"What do you think that is?" I ask Essna, and her eyes purposefully travel to my guards and stay there.

"Them, you are in love with your dragon guards. The only dragons in this world who you are forbidden to love, and yet, you fell. Why would we want a rebel who doesn't follow or respect rules to be our queen? Who would trust a princess who let a curse take her loves' dragons?" she asks, her voice echoing around the crowd, and everyone hears. I glance at my guards, who don't seem upset by her words like I am. If I could have stopped the curse, I would have. I never wanted the curse to take their dragons. I wouldn't wish that on anyone.

"I want to break the curse. The curse should never have been placed upon the guards," I say firmly.

"Yet, you are here to ask for help to take the

throne back. Which is it you want more, Isola Drag-ice? Your dragon guards free and the curse broken . . . or the throne," she asks, and I know she is testing me.

"Both," I answer.

"You cannot have everything in life. So, I will make you an offer. I will fight for you, and my army will side with you . . . only if you choose us over your guards. Make it clear to me that the throne means *everything* to you, and when you get it back, you will dedicate your entire life to fixing the mistakes of your father and his wife," she says, but the calculating smirk on her face tells me all I need to know. This isn't a real offer because she knows my answer, and she wants to drag it out for our audience.

"I will always fight for my dragon guards. I will always choose them. They are mine, and I am theirs," I state, walking up to the seer and not backing down. I'm their queen, not simply some stranger asking for help.

"The queen can only belong to the throne and the people it rules. A queen lost to her guards is no queen we want to follow or support," the seer responds, raising her hand, and I see several seers in cloaks walk over, surrounding us. Melody gives me a worried look, but my focus is on the little flash of silver I see at her hip as she steps closer to me.

"I am not asking. I am demanding," I say, and I reach across, sliding the dagger out from Melody's belt and holding it to my neck as shocked gasps fill the air.

"No, Isola, don't!" I hear Thorne shout. Growls emanate from my dragon guards as they fight their way over to me, but I don't look away from Essna. This is about me and her, nothing and no one else matters right now.

"I will use my last words to cast a curse, a curse on you that will make sure no one ever forgets the name Isola Dragice. I *am* the rightful queen, and I demand you give me fair trial to win your favour . . . or you should hope the magic is kind to you upon my death," I say, trying not to swallow with how nervous I am. Essna stares at me and finally lifts her hands into the air, stopping her people from coming near me. I wait for her people to move away, and I feel my dragon guards right behind me as I lower the dagger, holding it at my side.

"Impressive. There may be more to you yet, Isola Dragice," Essna says quietly, and stands up, raising her voice. "The princess is offered two trials for two prizes. The first will be the answer to breaking the dragon guard curse. The second will be to win our help in the war that she will bring to Dragca."

"What are the trials?" Melody asks Essna, who smiles like Melody is asking exactly what she wanted.

"On the blue moon in one week, she must enter the cave of memory. If she can make it to the other side, she will learn how to break the curse. The second trial will be on the yellow moon, three days after the blue moon, and you will not be told in advance what it entails," Essna tells me, and I glance at Melody, who shakes her head.

"This is unfair! No dragon has survived in the cave! Seers can barely make it through without losing their minds!" Melody exclaims, not exactly making me feel better about this cave. I watch as her eyes glaze over, and she stands very still. I think she is having a vision when suddenly her eyes pop open, and she stares right at me.

"She is no normal dragon, and she may take her light spirit with her. I'm sure she knows enough light magic that she will not miss the loss of her ice powers that the cave will take," Essna waves a hand as she speaks, and I finally look away from Melody.

"Make your choice," Essna says to me.

"I have one request first," I ask.

"Go on," Essna retorts, looking annoyed.

"My guards, my sister, and Darth are all to be treated as guests. Not as prisoners, and you must heal Korbin," I state, holding my hands on my hips, the dagger still in my hand.

"Korbin has been healed already. His parents have taken him," Essna says flippantly, and I try not to show the emotion on my face, though my relief is immense. "As for your other wishes, they are allowed as long as you take the trials. We are seers, and we look after those who we side with."

"Then I agree to your offer. I will take the trials," I say, knowing that I've likely just signed my death warrant. The cave of memory sounds like the last place I want to be or will be able to survive alone, without my powers.

"Can she take someone into the cave with her?" Thorne asks, stepping to my side, close enough that his arm brushes against mine.

"If anyone is going with Isola, it will be me or my brother. Not you," Elias snaps, pulling Thorne's shoulder, so he has to step back from my side as he shakes Elias off.

"Don't fight, now is not the time," I turn my head to whisper harshly at them as they glare at each other, clearly seconds away from fighting once again.

"No, the trial is for Isola only. She must do this alone," Essna snaps.

"I see him benefitting from travelling the cave. The past needs to be revealed; you should allow it," Melody says, and Essna narrows her eyes at her.

"You are not your mother. You are not even a full seer, so do not think you have the right to tell me what I should and should not do!" Essna practically growls, standing up.

"I meant no disrespect," Melody starts, but her expression says otherwise. "I only speak what the visions have shown me. He is meant to travel the cave with Isola. Thorne even feels the pull to his past, and that is why he is asking to go. We never *used* to ignore the visions that we are sent to guide us. I didn't realise things had changed so much since my mother was in charge." Essna's face narrows on Melody as people whisper in the crowds, and Melody simply smiles like she just won a prize at a circus.

"Nothing has changed. We still respect the magic of Dragca and trust in the visions she blesses us with," Essna snaps out, and slowly sighs as she glances at the people. "The fake king shall go with the princess. That is all for today." Essna quickly holds one hand in the air, and all the people copy her move.

"One more thing . . . is my uncle here?" I ask her, and she breathes out an aggrieved sigh again.

"No. He was, but he went to Earth to look for you. We haven't seen him in a while, but I'm sure he will return here when he realises you are no longer on Earth." She lowers her hand with her sharp words, and quickly walks away. The crowd all walk back to wherever they came from until there is just us, all standing together quietly. Jenny walks over, handing a key to me which I accept before she scurries off without a word. I quickly realise the key is for the handcuffs on my guards, and I turn to Thorne first.

"That was stupid. I could die in that cave, and now you might, too," I mutter angrily, undoing his cuffs which fall to the floor. Thorne catches my hand before I can turn away, making me look up at him. I hate how attractive he is, even with his blond hair all messy and littered with dirt and leaves. His stupidly perfect face stares down at me like I'm his everything, and all I can feel is anger. *And hate. I hate him, remember that Isola.*

"I've told you before, hate me all you want, but I

am *not* leaving your side. You will not die in that cave. We will get through it together, or I will at least make sure to find a way you will survive," he tells me, locking his eyes with mine and making me stare into those pale-blue eyes that remind me who he really is.

"Let's hope so, or Dragca will have no dragon heirs to the throne left to stop your mother," I pull away, and he lets me go, averting his eyes because he knows I am right. If we both die in that cave, there is no one left. I sigh as I rub my forehead, knowing things just got a million times more complicated. I walk over to Dagan and Elias who are talking quietly. Their conversation stops when I get to them, like that isn't suspicious at all. I raise my eyebrows at them, just as I notice something.

"I guess we all have a lot to talk about, but first, where is Bee?"

ELEVEN

ISOLA

"Bee is with Korbin. She didn't want to leave him alone. Darth went with them, and he said he would watch over her," Dagan tells me as I unlock his handcuffs after undoing Elias's. Dagan rubs his wrists, looking at me through his fringe, which has fallen into his face, and frowning. He gently places his hand on my cheek, rolling his lip ring around as I relax into his hand for a second. "It's going to be okay." Melody clears her throat, snapping me and Dagan out of the little moment we had.

"Do you know where Korbin is?" I ask. I want to see him, even if his parents are looking after him. I need to see that they have a cure, and if there is anything else I can do to help.

"Yep. In fact, his parents want to meet you," Elias grins. "Ready to meet the parents, naughty princess?"

"I didn't think of it like that, but erm, yes," I say, suddenly feeling nervous. What if they don't like me? What if they don't think I'm good enough for their son?

"They will love you," Melody says, clearly guessing what I'm thinking and smiling at me. "I'm going to sort out accommodations for us all and have a snoop around. I want to find out what the second trial will be. I don't like that she didn't tell us. Seers have many ways to kill dragons, and I'm not letting my sister go into an unfair trial." I smile at her words, loving how protective we have become over each other in such a short time.

"We shouldn't have split up. I don't trust everyone here not to try and kill us," I say before she can walk away from us.

"I will go with her," Thorne offers, stepping to Melody's side.

"Thanks," I tell him, only glancing his way briefly.

"Come on then, blondie," Melody says, not looking entirely happy about Thorne following after her, but I know she sees the reason in it. We can't trust this place, not yet.

"Princess Isola. Princess Isola's dragon guards," Jenny says from behind me, and I turn to see her standing behind me, bowing her head, and two other women stand next to her. I instantly scent that they are human, and when they lower their hoods, I believe they must be Jenny's children. The teenagers look like her, anyway. They have the same hair, similar features, and they give me a nervous glance.

"We wish for you to come with us and choose your weapons for the trials. I am also to take your guards to select new clothing to wear while they are here," she says, and Dagan places his hand on my shoulder as he steps to my side.

"I will choose the weapons for the princess and the clothes for myself, my brother, and Thorne," Dagan says, and I watch the two teenagers giggle as they stare at Dagan.

Kill, nice meal these humans, my dragon growls, pushing for me to shift.

No! Dagan looks like a god, you can't blame them for finding him hot, I try to reason with her, and she huffs.

"Everything okay?" Dagan asks me, snapping me out of my head. I turn to him, leaning up and kissing him thoroughly, loving how his lip ring pushes against my lips.

"Everything is fine, my dragon was just getting a little jealous," I admit to him, forgetting that there is anyone else here as Dagan slides his hand to the back of my head and takes my lips passionately. His lips press against mine, marking me, and making me completely unaware of anything other than his kiss until he breaks away.

"There is nothing to be jealous of," he whispers against my lips, the chill from his lip ring a direct opposite of his warm lips. It feels amazing, and I wish we were alone.

"I wouldn't say that," Elias drawls from my other side as Dagan and I break away and see Jenny narrowing her eyes at me with her hands on her hips.

"Young people, always frolicking. Come on with me if you think you can manage to pry yourself away from the princess, Mr. Fire," Jenny scolds, and I try not to laugh at her annoyed face as she turns, walking away with her daughters trailing behind her. Dagan winks at me before following her, and I turn to Elias, who holds out a hand. I slide my hand into his, and he pulls me close to his side as we walk across the clearing towards a path in the trees. I look over at two women watching us near a table as they fold clothes. I still see the look of desire they flash Elias. The growl slips from my lips before I can stop it, and they jump, giving me a fearful look before scampering away.

"That's not the way to make friends, princess," Elias laughs.

"My dragon is a little possessive," I reply, not apologising for it. They could clearly see us close together and should have figured out he is off limits.

"Mine, too," he kisses the side of my head. "But yours has nothing to worry about." I don't answer him, knowing nothing is really certain between any of us, and that's why my dragon worries. She won't stop being jealous and irrational until mating with them. Dragons are naturally territorial of what they think of as theirs. Unfortunately for me, my dragon thinks sexy guys are like jewels. And she wants to hoard them all, keeping them for herself.

"How is your arm?" he asks, and I automatically glance at it. It's really weird how you have to look when someone asks about something.

"It's okay, I don't think it will be long before I can take it off," I answer. It is feeling a lot better. I will be glad to take the bandage off later.

"You were amazing today, you know that?" he

says, watching as two seers pass us, not even looking our way.

"I don't think amazing is the right word to describe it. I haven't gotten any of them on my side or believing in me," I respond quietly. "How did my father and my family before him just get people to follow them?" I ask the question I keep wondering. I know one of my ancestors won a war and that made him king, but how did my family never get kicked off the throne until now? I know we are stronger than fire dragons, but there are only so many of us, and every generation there are less. I always wondered what would have happened if I had a child with Jace and who that child would have mated with. With no ice heirs, it would have had to be a fire dragon, and then everyone would find out that fire and ice dragons can have children together like Thorne. Fire was always heading towards the throne, one way or another. My father wasn't a stupid man, he would have thought this all through, so what was his plan?

"By being a leader, a ruler. By being a light they could follow when it felt like darkness was all that was left," he tells me. I don't reply as we follow the path, walking past more huts until we are quite far out in the woods.

"How do you *become* a leader?" I ask, because it's clear I do not have a clue.

"By being inspirational," he shrugs. "I always used to hear tales of the king and queen, and how even though they had their issues, they were inspirational to see."

"Then this is hopeless. I'm not an inspiration to anyone. I'm a princess of a world I wasn't even brought up in, a princess that let her father be killed and then forgot who she was. A princess that didn't even *want* the throne in the first place," I say, starting to panic as everything collapses in on me. What the hell am I doing trying to get the throne back? Why aren't I running away like a smart person would? Elias pulls me to him, tucking my head under his chin as I try to calm down. When it becomes hard to breathe, I start to panic more, not knowing what is happening to me.

"You're having a panic attack. Breathe nice and slow and listen to me talk. Just listen and think of nothing else," Elias says calmly, trying to soothe me, but it doesn't work. I just feel like I can't breathe, and everything I don't want to remember or think about is rushing through my mind.

"I-I can't do this," I breathe out, my words catching and likely not making any sense.

"Isola Dragice, you know what I thought when I first met you?" he asks as I try to take deep breaths and just relax in his smoky scent.

"No," I shakily exhale.

"I thought, 'wow, she is pretty gorgeous'. Then a few hours later I thought, 'wow, she is going to die super quick because she is so clueless'," he says, and it makes me laugh a little.

"If you're trying to make me feel better, you suck at it," I eventually say, loving the soothing circles he rubs into my back with his thumb.

"It took one week for me to know I was absolutely wrong about you. So wrong. I saw how strong you are, how kind, and how utterly special. Isola Dragice walked straight into a world she could barely remember, clueless and heartbroken . . . and held her head high even when everything was stacked against her," he pauses, lifting my chin, so we are looking at each other. "If that isn't inspirational, I don't know what else is. Everything you have been through, everything you have lost, and you are still standing here. That alone is amazing. You still fight for what is right when we both know it would be easier to run away."

"Why do you believe in me so much?" I question quietly.

"Because I love you," he whispers, and my eyes widen in shock as I just gape, momentarily at a loss for words. "Because I've loved you, an inspirational girl I met once as a boy, since you gave me that second chance at life. I spent years dreaming about her, even when I discovered she was the princess, and I knew she would never look at me twice. I love you because you never gave up on me, not once, even when I didn't know who you were. I love you, Isola Dragice, and I will always be yours."

"I love you, too," I whisper, and lean up, pressing my lips against his, only able to do it once before he loses all control and slams his lips firmly on mine and picks me up in his arms. Elias walks us through the trees, away from anyone or any path, as we fervently kiss each other. I pull his shirt off when he stops, and he slowly slides me down his body, gently biting my bottom lip before letting go and stepping back.

"I want to see you, all of you," he tells me, and I nervously unclip my cloak, letting it fall to the ground. I pull my top off, careful not to hurt my arm, and watch as Elias's eyes widen and fill with heat. I wriggle out of my trousers as I scan my eyes over Elias's chest, the dragon tattoo, the words on his heart, and finally down to the trail of dark hair that disappears into his jeans. I look up as my trousers fall to the floor, and I step out of them, standing completely bare in front of him. When I meet his eyes and see the desire, any embarrassment disappears as I see how much he wants me. How nothing he sees is anything other than what he wants, what he needs.

"I'm yours, Elias. Isn't it about time you show me what it's like to belong to Elias Fire?" I whisper, and my words make him snap, taking one big step forward and picking me up. Elias lies me down on my clothes, holding my uninjured hand above my head as he keeps eye contact with me and presses his body against mine. Even with his jeans on, the friction makes me gasp as he knocks my legs apart. Elias slowly kisses down my jaw, pausing to graze his teeth against a sensitive part on my neck before moving lower. I moan as his lips find my nipple, sucking it into his mouth and biting down gently. The mixture of both pleasure and pain drives me crazy until he breaks away and spends time with my other breast.

"Isola, you are so fucking beautiful," Elias comments between kisses as he makes his way down my body until he finds where he was looking for.

"Eli," I moan as his talented tongue finds my core and starts twirling in slow, perfect circles that get me so close, but aren't quite enough to push me over the edge. The asshole is teasing me.

"Enough, I want you now," I say, and he lifts his head, seductively licking his lips as he looks down at me.

"Are you sure you can handle me?" he asks with an amused grin as I slip my hands to his jeans, undoing the button and sliding my hand inside. Elias's grin disappears when I wrap my hand around him, stroking him firmly and making him groan as he closes his eyes.

"Are you sure you can handle me?" I mimic him, and his eyes leisurely open as his hand grabs mine, pulling me away only to maneuver his body on top of mine.

"No, I know you are going to drive me insane when I'm inside of you. You already do just when we kiss," he tells me and kisses me, stopping anymore talking. I kick his jeans down his legs, writhing against him as his hands explore my breasts and his lips devour my own. I gasp as Elias thrusts into me, every inch of him feeling amazing as he slowly fills me up.

"Eli, I love you, don't stop," I mumble out

around kisses, arching my back as Elias kisses my neck and groans loudly as he slams into me again and again.

"I won't. God, you're everything," he says, leaning up and kissing me roughly as he picks up his pace. I moan as an orgasm unexpectedly slams into me, and Elias bites my neck, speeding up his thrusts until I feel him finish. We both lie together, our foreheads resting against each other, and our heavy breathing is the only sound.

"It's impossible how much I love you," he whispers, and I smile as I whisper back.

"Nothing is impossible."

"Okay, are there any more leaves in my hair?" I ask Elias after shaking my hair out once again. I don't want to meet Korbin's parents with flushed cheeks and messy hair that is full of dirt and leaves. They will know straight away from our scent alone, but I'm not hiding my relationship from anyone. I couldn't even if I tried. The whole camp must be talking about how I basically claimed my dragon guards when Essna asked me to choose them or the throne. Starting off on a lie isn't the best way to do anything. Elias chuckles, pulling his shirt on and walking over to me. He reaches a hand into my hair and pulls out a leaf.

"Just the one, and now you're perfect," he grins,

making me laugh. Elias helps me clip my cloak on, and I'm just about to start walking back to the path when he speaks.

"I was worried what happened with the Earth boy would affect us. You would tell me if I scared you, right?" I turn at his unsure voice and walk straight up to him, placing my hands on his chest.

"You could never scare me. I didn't think about–" I have to clear my throat before I can say his name, "Michael. What he almost did, well, it's not going to ruin my life. Do I get scared sometimes? Yes. But never when I'm with any of you. I know I'm safe, that you'd never hurt me, so I don't need to be scared." I stop rambling when he kisses me, and I can feel the smile on his lips before I even see it.

"You're *always* safe with us. I'm glad you know that," he replies, linking our hands together, and we walk through the forest. We are silent for most of the walk once we get back on the path and pass a few huts with people milling around. Most of them stare, and a few children run past us as they sing songs with big smiles on their faces.

"The people look so happy here," I say quietly.

"Yes. I know the fire rebellion was once a group of dragons, seers, and humans that believed in the old ways of Dragca to guide them. They trusted light and dark magic, fire and ice, and all that Dragca naturally gave to them. Your father did not hold those same beliefs. He did not think dark magic should be respected, or even practised. I don't believe he trusted magic of any kind, purely because I heard of many missions where guards were sent to find and stop practisers," he says. I rest my head on his shoulder as I look at the children and their mother watching them from the door with a big smile on her lips. How could my father destroy people for loving Dragca and magic?

"Why would he hunt light magic users? It makes no sense, as far as I know you cannot use it for anything, and the only magic we've known for years is dark and destructive," I say, thinking back to the stories Jace told me about. He said his parents told him that dark magic had taken over a farm boy, and he had killed an entire village by accident. His parents told him that story when he was twelve, and three weeks later they disappeared. We never did find out where they went, but Jace always said he felt like they were alive somewhere, though I'm pretty sure they are dead.

"Lies. I know others were connected to the light magic, but not on a scale like you are and like Tatarina is to dark. They didn't get spirits and the protection from that. They could just use it for tiny things, like healing plants and making light," he says tensely. "Nothing that could hurt someone, not like what you are capable of."

"Did you see Tatarina a lot in the dungeons? Did you see her use dark magic to hurt someone?" I ask, because we haven't had time to talk about where he was and what happened during those years I didn't know he existed. It couldn't have been easy, even with Thorne protecting them for me.

"Yes. She liked to use her dark magic on us and the other prisoners, who she regularly killed by accident. I believe it made her stronger, and her dark spirit, Nane, enjoyed watching," he answers. I know he is hiding the worst of it from me, and I squeeze his hand tightly, letting him know he can talk to me whenever he wants to. *When did we all become so broken?*

"I don't think we can kill Nane, not without killing Bee. I've heard several times now that there must be dark and light alive at the same time. I worry that destroying one, will destroy the other," I whisper, but he hears me. I won't let Bee die, not for anything. I'm too attached to the little green Barbie doll that eats like a horse and, I'm pretty sure, likes food more than me.

"I don't know enough of light and dark magic to advise you. I just know that Nane must be controlled if she is kept alive. Also, she won't survive without a new host, not if you kill Tatarina," he tells me, and I suspected as much.

"Let's hope Nane's next choice is better than her first, or we will just end up killing one host after another, and that isn't something I want to do," I admit, and we both walk in silence to the end of the path where a large hut sits. The hut is two put together, but I imagine they make one house. There is smoke coming out of the hole in the middle of the main part of the hut, and I can hear quiet talking inside.

"Time to meet the parents," Elias teases me with a big grin on his lips, and I roll my eyes at him as we walk to the door. I lift my hand, knocking twice. The door is opened a few seconds later by Darth, who smiles when he sees us. He has a few cuts on his face that are stitched up, his grey hair looks brushed, and he has new clothes on, with a long cloak clipped at his neck. They have been looking after him, but I still feel a little bad about dropping him in the forest and cutting his face. Hopefully, they won't scar.

"It's about time you got here, girl," he says, and

holds the door open as I walk in, and he shuts the door behind us.

"I'm glad you're okay after the fall," I reply with a smile.

"I was lucky to land in a rather large pond with Korbin and Elias. We swam out, carrying Korbin of course, and then the seers found us," he says and points at his face as he chuckles, "though I managed to hit a few sharp rocks under the water somehow. I've always been a little unlucky."

"You were lucky my son was found right then. I doubt he would have survived much longer in the state he was in," a woman says, stepping through a fabric curtain in the room and standing still, assessing me and Elias. The woman is stunning, with long black hair in braids, light-brown skin and green eyes that are the image of Korbin's eyes. Even without her saying anything, I would have known she was his mother, or at least a close relative.

"That was not my fault, Janiya," Darth says, shaking his head.

"You should have called me straight away, father! He is my only son, and if he had died, there would be nothing left!" Janiya shouts, fire lighting up her arms as her eyes turn black, and she looks away sharply as she calms herself down. I stare at Darth with my mouth gaping open.

"You're Kor's grandfather?" Elias is the one that speaks before I can.

"Yes, not that we ever met. I was a terrible father, always working. Janiya joined the dragon guard when she turned eighteen to escape," he explains.

"That's not the only reason I joined, father; not everything is about you," Janiya huffs, and Darth smiles indulgently at her.

"You are just as stubborn as your mother," he says, and shakes his head. "I will leave you to meet the woman your son is in love with." Darth says, walking around us and out of the door as I lock eyes with Janiya.

"Princess Isola Dragice, I presume?" Janiya says, crossing her arms and making the bangles on them clang against each other. It's only then that I notice she has a dragon guard uniform on, a purple cloak and three metal, circular necklaces around her neck that match the bangles on her arms.

"Yes, it is nice to meet you," I say as I step forward and hold a hand out for her to shake. Janiya stares at my hand before sliding hers into it, gripping me tightly.

"Thank you for keeping my son alive for as long as you and your guards did," she says tightly, like it pains her to thank me. She stares at my eyes for a long time, seeming like she has just seen a ghost or something as she whispers under her breath. "You look just like your father."

"It's nothing, I would never have let him die, and thank you. I've always heard I have my father's eyes, but I look like my mother," I say, pulling my hand away and glancing through a small gap in the curtain, seeing Korbin on a bed.

"No, your mother had a kind face and your father was more . . . determined. You will find you are much more of your father than your mother, Isola Dragice," she says, shaking her head.

"I don't think it matters who I am most like in looks, I know I am different to them both. More importantly though, I came to see Korbin. I need to know if he is okay," I say, stepping closer to the fabric and the gap where I can see Korbin sleeping.

"Unfortunately, I don't wish for you to see my son anymore. You will cause his death, and I won't allow that," Janiya says, stepping in front of the gap and glaring at me as she crosses her arms again.

"You can't stop me," I state firmly, crossing my own arms and holding my ground.

"I *will* stop you if that's what it takes, but instead, hopefully, you can be reasoned with. You are the princess, a princess that over half of this world is looking to kill or dedicate to a throne for the rest of your life. If my son is at your side, he will die protecting you, or worse, be used against you. Have you even thought about the risk of having my son at your side? If you care about him at all, you will walk away," she asserts, making me question my own decision until I remember that I can't make Korbin stay away from me. Even if I walked away, he would still protect me, and he could die at any point because life isn't certain. Death is, but how we live our lives should be our choice. I won't make that choice for Korbin. He knows the risk of being with me.

"Janiya, love, enough of this. We have talked about our son's decisions, and you know what he wants," a man says firmly, after stepping out of the curtain and standing next to her. The man looks like an older version of Korbin as they share a lot of facial features, but he has light-brown hair, tanned golden skin, and kind-looking brown eyes.

"Phelan, this is insane. He can't mate with her! That would make a dragon guard a king, and no one will ever accept that! So, what is the point of letting them be together? She will get our son killed! Royals get everyone killed, and besides, her father killed my mother!" she growls out, pushing Phelan away and slamming her shoulder into mine as she passes me and walks out of the hut.

"I didn't know what my father did," I whisper into the silence of the room. No wonder she hates me. My father killed her mother, and in her eyes, I'm now trying to get her son killed.

"We cannot be held accountable for the actions of our parents. I am sorry for my mate's reaction. She just fears for Korbin's life, and things have been touch and go for the last two days. I don't think she has slept since he came back," he explains.

"I understand that. If I could walk away from him, I would have done so by now. I can't, and ultimately, it is up to Korbin who he chooses to love and fight for," I say gently.

"My son has told me all about you, and I know there isn't a chance in Dragca that he is leaving your side," he chuckles. "You can thank his mother for his stubbornness. They are very much alike and are usually butting heads over something."

"Why did my father kill Korbin's grandmother?" I ask.

"I do not know everything, only that Janiya's

mother knew something, something she shouldn't have known. The dragon guards were sent in the night, and they murdered Janiya's mother while Janiya was training in the dragon guard. She found out the next morning and left the guard with me, running to the only place where the king couldn't track us. The fire rebellion," he tells us, and I glance at Elias, who looks as confused as I am.

"I don't understand. How did my father ever trust you two again? I mean, you are dragon guards."

"He didn't know who we were, we changed our names, and your father had long forgotten Janiya over the years of hunting her. When you run from the curse, it does eventually give up on chasing you. The magic isn't endless, and the king had many runaways to deal with. When Korbin was old enough, we knew he had to return because of the curse. We followed him back, became the best dragon guards your father had, and Korbin got the training he needed," he clarifies.

"Still, I am sorry for what my father did," I say and look away, "I seem to be apologizing for a lot of his actions recently. I didn't have a clue who he really was and what he did as king."

"Just be different than he was, that's all any of us want. Tatarina is very much like her departed husband, and no one wants her on the throne. Make good choices," he says, and pats my shoulder before walking to the door.

"Where is Bee?" I ask, making him pause and look back. "In the kitchen, which is at the back of the hut through that curtain. I found her a bunch of human chocolate and sweets, and she has ignored us since. Now, I better go find my mate," he grins, one much like his son's, before walking out. I walk to the right, peeking through the open curtain and seeing Korbin fast asleep on his side. One leg sticks out of the blanket, and his light snores fill the room.

"Let's check on Bee before we wake him. He looks comfy," I whisper to Elias who peers over my head at Korbin.

"Sure," Elias replies, and I step back, walking across the little living room in the hut. There are sofas in here, a fireplace, and brightly coloured, worn rugs on the floor. There is a makeshift wall at the back of the hut, made out of a purple, nearly see through fabric. I move it aside and walk in, laughing at the sight that greets me. Bee is on a table, lying in a glass bowl full of bubbly water, sunbathing from the beam of light coming in from the window. There are dozens of wrappers from sweets and chocolate all around the bowl, and Bee is currently trying to eat a chocolate bar that is bigger than her head, as it melts in the water.

"Bee?" I ask, hearing Elias chuckle behind me. Bee drops the bar into the water, flashing me a chocolate-covered grin.

"You back," she says, and I sigh.

"I missed you too, Bee. I need to train on how to use light tomorrow. You can rest, or do whatever it is you are doing now, but tomorrow, things have to change. I need to be able to use the light to survive now," I say, and she yawns, looking unimpressed.

"Good," she says, pushing her green hair out of her face and picking up her chocolate bar, clearly done with our conversation.

"Are you sure you are ready to use light magic?" Elias asks as we walk out of the small kitchen.

"No, but then again, I don't think I have a choice. This is who I am meant to be, and Dragca needs magic once again."

CHAPTER

THIRTEEN

ISOLA

"Hey, sleepy head," I call softly, stroking the side of Korbin's face. His green eyes open slowly as he jolts up, relaxing back into the pillow when he sees it's me. Korbin looks amazing, so much better than he was. The purple lines are gone, his skin has colour, and he looks, well, more alive.

"What is a sleepy head? It sounds kind of dirty," Elias asks from where he is leaning against the wall.

"It's an expression. It just means you have sleepy, cute, messy hair. Don't worry, you look cuter in the morning. I think Korbin has the sexy look instead," I wink at him, and he growls.

"I'm *not* cute. I'd rather be sexy. Sexy tops cute,"

Elias grumbles as Korbin and I laugh. Korbin sits himself up on the bed, only flinching in pain slightly before relaxing back against the wooden headboard. He coughs a few times, and I place my hand in his, trying not to show how worried I still am about him.

"I'm fine, honest. I just could do with a glass of water," he says, and I go to get up, but he holds my hand tightly. "I can wait, though, I'd rather you stay with me."

"I'll get it, man," Elias says in understanding before I can reply, walking out of the room.

"How did they heal you?" I ask, curious. Korbin pulls his shirt up, showing me the purple leaves stuck over the cut.

"There is a plant called Tunits, and their leaves absorb anything. They are rare in Dragca, and the leaves are expensive to buy. Of course, my parents sent for the leaves the moment the seers brought me here. Darth helped heal me with your blood until the leaves could be found," Korbin explains.

"You know Darth is your grandfather?" I ask, and he chuckles.

"Yeah, I was shocked at first. The old dragon is good at keeping secrets, and I can't scent him because . . ." he stops, pain flickering in his eyes at the mention of losing his dragon, and I squeeze his hand. "Anyway, my mum slapped the silly out of him when he first walked in here."

"Your mum is erm . . . scary," I say, and he laughs loudly, holding his stomach as laughing must hurt him.

"You braved my parents to come and see me? I'm impressed you made it in here," Korbin comments.

"Actually, it was just your mum I had to brave. Your dad seemed to be okay with me," I tell him, shrugging, and he laughs, even though it seems to hurt him a little.

"They will love you, just like I do. It will just take time. Especially if you ever answer that question I asked you before Eli came in," he says with a nervous grin on his lips. There are a million reasons why I should say no. Responsibility of the throne. The timing. The fact I haven't spoken to Elias or Dagan about all this. Yet, there is one reason I know all that stuff doesn't matter. I want Korbin as my mate. I nearly watched him die, and I know my life would be empty without him.

"You know my answer, it was always yes," I whisper timidly, and he grins, tugging me down with his one hand, so he can kiss me. I break away just as Elias comes into the room, but I can't look away from Korbin and the massive smile on his face. I lean forward and kiss Kor again, grazing my lips against his, and he laughs, gently holding me back.

"I love you, too," he says with a chuckle. "But remember I'm not well enough to really show you how much."

"Don't stop on my account," Elias says playfully, coming over and handing Korbin the drink. Korbin drinks most of it before handing it to me, and I hop off the bed, so I can reach the dresser to put the glass of water on top.

"Isola just agreed to mate with me," Kor suddenly blurts out, and I turn, giving him a wide-eyed look that suggests he stop talking, but he doesn't seem to get it. He shrugs his shoulders and explains. "Almost dying made me realise I love her more than anything, and I don't want to wait years to make a decision when I know what I want. We could be killed any day, and Isola is it for me. Thank god, she said yes."

"What? Don't you think that is something we all should discuss?" Elias exclaims, and I turn in time to see him run his hands through his hair.

"I'm not taking her from you. I would never stop

her from also mating with you or Dagan. I just need Isola to know how I feel about her. I know how serious mating is, and we have made our choice. I want you to accept it. It was you that suggested the idea of sharing and all of us being together in the first place," Kor says. *When was this conversation?*

"But being mated . . . that's something else. I never thought that far ahead," Elias mutters, flashing me a guilty look when he finally looks my way and likely sees all my emotions on my face. *He . . . he doesn't want me?*

"Are you saying you never see yourself mating to me?" I ask quietly, and Elias shakes his head, walking over to me and trying to reach for my hands, but I jerk back away from him.

"It's not that, it's just mating is forever. It's a blessing and a big step. We are young and–" I cut him off as I don't want to hear it. He was just telling me how much he loved me, and we were having sex, but *now* he isn't sure? He certainly wasn't unsure when he was inside of me. Why are men such assholes sometimes?

"You know what, Eli? Just get out, or I'm going to leave," I shout, my words coming out a growl as my dragon's anger fills me, making everything seem doubly as painful. I step back, hearing a cracking noise, and I look down to see the floor around me is frozen, the ice spreading towards Eli and Kor's bed.

"Isola . . ." Eli starts, but I can't look up at him as I try to stop the ice. It doesn't work, instead the room starts snowing. As snow falls on my cheeks, I look up to see Eli just standing there, looking bewildered as snow covers him.

"Leave, just please leave. You're right, I didn't think any of this through. Me, you, Kor, and Dagan. How can we possibly all get blessed and be mated when it's clear you never even *thought* about being that serious with me?" I ask, my heart pounding in my ears in fear of anything Elias might say.

"Isola, it's not that I don't love you–" he starts to say, and I shake my head, the snow falling inside the room increasing.

"You just don't want to mate with me, I get it. Now get out," I say quietly.

"Isola–"

"Just get out!" I shout, covering my face with my hands, and my voice trailing off into a whisper. "Please go. I can't deal with this right now."

"Leave, Elias. Don't make me try and get off this bed to kick you out. You've said enough for today, don't you think?" Kor says firmly as I stare at the wall and try not to cry. I hear Elias walk out of the room and the sound of the door slamming only moments later.

"Come here, doll," Korbin gently coaxes, and I run over, burying my head into his neck as he drapes an arm around my waist.

"Elias is scared, you know that, right? He's scared of losing you, and I bet he thinks mating with you will kill him more if he lost you. I know he loves you, and whatever is stopping him from mating with you, it is in his head. It's fear, not lack of love," he tells me soothingly, but nothing seems to help with how my heart feels like it is shattering.

"I get being scared, I'm scared every day, but I don't get not wanting or planning a future with the people I love," I whisper, my words not making much sense as I wipe my tears on Kor's shirt.

"I know, doll. Give Elias time to calm down. His shock over you agreeing to mate with me, everything that is going on, and losing his dragon is messing with his head. Give him time," he says.

"He shouldn't have to think whether he wants me or not. I never had to think like that about any of you. I just knew, deep down inside, I knew," I reply.

"Me, too, doll," Korbin says, kissing the top of my head. "Stay with me for a while? I could do with holding you close."

"I'm not going anywhere," I mumble, wiping the tears off my face and relaxing in Korbin's arms. *If Elias doesn't want me, fine, but I'm not going to allow it to destroy me and distract me from the trials. I can't, because if I'm destroyed, what becomes of Dragca?*

FOURTEEN

"These are the huts they have given us to live in while we are here. I think someone should stay on guard, and no one should be alone anyway. I don't trust Essna. There is something else going on here," Melody says, waving a hand at the two huts in front of us, but keeping her serious eyes on me until I sharply nod. I don't trust Essna either. I look back at the huts, seeing that one is massive and looks like it could fit dozens of people inside. The one next to it is rather small. Bee flies off my shoulder, flying into the hut through a gap in the fabric before I can stop her. She wasn't pleased that we had to leave Kor at his parents' and with Darth until he is better. I can't say I'm happy about it, but I know he isn't well enough to be moved yet, and his parents will care for him. I also know I need to start training as soon as possible with Bee, and I'm going to be distracted until the trials.

"I will check it is safe first," Dagan says, walking past me and through the fabric door. I roll my eyes over his black trousers and shirt, and the two swords on his hips attached to his belt in holders. He also has a new dark-blue cloak which he holds rather than wears. It isn't cold, and I might take my cloak off soon as it feels like the middle of summer here. I aimlessly look around the trees surrounding the huts, noticing that they have put us far away from anyone else. I don't know if that's to protect us or them. More likely them.

"Where is Thorne?" I ask, remembering that he was supposed to be with Melody for protection.

"With Elias getting food for us all. We bumped into him on the way back here," she explains.

"That's good," I say tightly, even hearing his name makes my dragon growl, and my heart pound in my chest.

"What's up? You've looked like someone killed your puppy since you left Korbin's," Melody says, nudging me with her shoulder.

"I don't have a puppy," I reply dryly, really not wanting to talk about anything.

"It's a metaphor, now come on, out with it," she demands, and I'm thankful for the distraction when Dagan comes out of the hut.

"It's clear, come on in. It's actually pretty nice," he calls to us, holding the fabric door open. I quickly walk in, happy to get away from Melody and her questioning gaze. The hut is nice, with three red sofas and a matching red and yellow woven rug in the middle of them. There is a fireplace, which is already lit and makes the room really warm. I see five doors, and I'm guessing they lead to the bedrooms, bathroom, and kitchen areas.

"I'm taking the hut next door. It's made for one, anyway, and I want to watch my orb for a while," she says, placing her hand on my arm for a second.

"You could stay here," I say.

"No, it's yours, and there are some things a sister never wants to hear through these thin straw walls," Melody pulls a disgusted face and walks back out of the door as I smile. She has a point, or at least I hope she does. I walk into the room, sitting on the couch and laying my head back, staring at the ceiling.

"What happened? Did Kor upset you? His parents say something?" Dagan asks, moving to the back of the sofa and looking down at me, rolling that lip ring around. I stare up at him, noticing how long his hair has gotten in the last couple of weeks. Dagan usually keeps it short, and it needs a cut, but the dark-brown, wavy hair makes him look dangerously sexy.

"Nothing happened," I mutter, standing up and walking to the fireplace, looking at the little wooden dragon statue in the middle of the mantle. I pick it up, smoothing my hands over the wood and thinking of the detail that must have gone into making it.

"What the hell happened, kitty cat? Talk to me," Dagan asks, and the fabric door opens, with Elias and Thorne walking in as I stiffen up. My eyes immediately lock with Elias, seeing the guilt and maybe even fear in his eyes as he stops and stares at me. I don't seem to be able to focus on anyone else, or anything going on in the room other than Elias.

"Leave me alone with Isola. I'm the one that pissed her off because I'm an idiot, and we need to talk," Elias says, looking awkward as I glare at him.

"Sure," Thorne agrees, putting the bags on the floor next to the ones Elias put down. "But if you hurt her, you're dead," Thorne says calmly, but with just enough protective tones that it sends shivers through me. Elias doesn't look his way, keeping his eyes on me the whole time.

"Fix whatever stupid shit you said. We need to be united at the moment, not apart," Dagan whispers adamantly to Elias as he passes him, but Elias still keeps his eyes locked on mine. In the corner of my eye, I see Dagan pat Thorne's shoulder, before practically pushing him out of the door.

"You don't need to apologise. I've had time to think about it. If you think I'm not worth mating with, if you don't want me for more than just fun, then I will break the dragon guards' curse, and you can leave," I say as I turn away, annoyed when my voice catches when I try so hard to be emotionless. Elias walks over, taking my face into his hands and holding on tightly. He forces me to look into his eyes that show his every emotion, and all I can see is fear. He is scared.

"I love you. I fucking *love* you, and everything I said about mating, it had nothing to do with how I feel about you," he growls.

"Then I don't get it, am I not enough? Do you never want to mate with anyone?" I ask, and his thumb wipes a tear away that falls down my right cheek.

"I am scared, not of mating and you, but of being

a disappointment to you. Mating with you would make me a king, would make me a leader, and I'm definitely not that. I can't be what you need, and I don't want you to mate with me, then regret it down the line," he admits, his voice quiet like he doesn't want to tell me this.

"I would never regret that. I would never regret *you*," I breathe out.

"Yes, you would. People will never accept that you have more than one mate, let alone all of them being dragon guards, Isola. Mating with you, it could ruin everything, and I don't want to risk that. We can be together as much as we want, without me being a king," he says gently, almost like he's trying to soothe me, but I don't agree with a single word he says.

"The people need a queen who isn't cruel, isn't dead inside, and isn't lost. If I don't have all of you as my mates, if I have to give you up for the throne, I might as well leave Tatarina on it. They would not have a better leader if I were destroyed. Dragca is changing, and it will change with me. I want you as my mate, and I don't care what anyone else, other than you, thinks. If you care about the opinions of strangers more than me, then there is nothing worth fighting for between us," I pull away from him, walking over to one of the doors as he lets me go.

"Make your choice. I won't make anyone love me, mate with me, or be with me if they are scared of what that means. You have always known who I am and the price that comes with being with me. If we have no future, please tell me now and don't break my heart any more than you already have," I watch as he tensely watches me speak, never moving, and I know I have to get away from him before he sees me break down. I turn and open the nearest door, which leads to a small bedroom. Quickly closing the door behind me, I slide down the door, finally letting the tears fall.

FIFTEEN

ISOLA

"Isola? Elias?" I hear shouted, making me sit up from where I've been slumped on the floor in the tiny bedroom for god knows how long. My dragon whines as I stand up, stretching my arms and wiping my dry lips. It's funny how time seems to stop when your heart is breaking. I feel like I've already lost Eli in a way, and what's worse, I'm more broken than when I lost Jace. How could I love Eli more than Jace, when I knew Jace nearly my entire life? The only conclusion I come to is that I'm a crappy person, and Eli is likely better off without me. Then in the next thought, I'm furious at Eli and think I need to woman up. *Or princess up? I actually have no clue.*

"I'm in here," I shout back, not even remembering who called until Dagan opens the door and, at seeing my face, closes it behind him in one smooth motion. He steps into the room and pulls me into his arms. I tense up for second, but when his smoky scent hits me, it relaxes me as well as my dragon.

"I'm okay," I whisper, feeling how tense he is as my head rests against his chest.

"Elias is in a room with the door locked, and I'm betting he is regretting whatever the hell he said. I don't want you to tell me what happened, but I do want you for the night. Let me take you out somewhere," he asks. "A date, because we haven't actually had a real one."

"We went to the café in the rain and had sandwiches, that's totally a date," I tease him, and he chuckles.

"Eating those horrendous sandwiches is not a date. Plus, this is Dragca, not Earth. I want to take you on a date in our world," he says.

"Where? We can't leave . . ." I trail off as he pulls back from me a little, so he can see my face as I look up at him.

"Trust me?" he asks, kissing my forehead.

"You know I do," I chuckle, and he steps back with a big grin, linking our hands and walking us out of the room. Thorne is sitting on the sofa, sharpening a sword while Bee sleeps on the sofa next to him. She even has Thorne's dark-blue cloak covering her. Thorne looks up, but I can't focus on anything other than the fact he doesn't have a shirt on. Holy crap, he has nice abs. There are eight of them, covered in sweat, and his man nipples even look attractive. *Oh god, now I can't stop thinking about licking man nipples. I don't even know if that is what you call them, or how they can be attractive, but his are.* Thorne flashes me a smile and flips his sword over in his large hands as his wavy blonde hair falls into his face.

"Isola?" Dagan's amused voice calls, snapping me out of my drooling, and I physically have to close my mouth. Why are all these dragon guards built like damn gods? It's so unfair and distracting. I can't even manage to collect my thoughts until I look away.

"Have a good night," is all Thorne says, looking back down at his sword and going back to what he was doing. I look back at the doors in the room for a distraction. Knowing Elias is behind one of them just makes me sad, and it's worse that he didn't come to me, but in a way I'm glad he didn't go far. Maybe he doesn't want me anymore? I try to redirect my thoughts, forget everything going on, and focus on where Dagan is taking me. We walk out of the hut together and see that the lanterns are all lit, lighting up the dark forest, so you can only see them. I look up, seeing the outline of the two moons and the dozens of stars lighting up the sky.

"What kind of dates do you go on in Dragca usually?" I ask Dagan, who tugs me closer, wrapping an arm around my waist as we walk.

"I think it depends on the girl. If I could take you anywhere, it would be to the biggest library in Dragca. There are thousands of books in there, both modern and old. It's amazing, and I would take you to a nice meal, then of course back to my place for dessert," he tells me, and I chuckle.

"I like the sound of your date," I grin mischievously, and he laughs. "But I will admit I'm slightly jealous of the previous girls that went on dates with you."

"I never really got to date while growing up, to be honest with you," he tells me.

"Why?" I ask, glancing up at him as he watches the forest as we walk.

"Well, I had to train, and then Elias was always getting into shit. I was the one getting him out of trouble all the time or taking the blame, so I would get stuck with extra training on our days off," he says.

"That must have been crap," I say.

"Maybe. Maybe not. I'm a pretty amazing fighter now because of it, and Elias isn't dead like he would have been if I hadn't helped him. Either way, it all worked out for the best because I'm here with you," he says, tilting his head down and to the side slightly as he watches my reaction.

"So, you wouldn't change anything?" I ask.

"No. There is only one thing about my past I wish I could know," he says with a sigh.

"About your father?" I guess.

"Yes. We didn't know who he was, and we never knew if he had family. Sisters. Brothers . . . just nothing. Our mum was so heartbroken she wouldn't say a thing, and we were too young to remember," he explains.

"Sometimes, you have to accept you can't know everything you want to," I whisper. "If I could know why my father did the things he did. If I could know why he sent you guys to me, why he never told me about Melody, or told me about anything important . . . well, it would change my life," I say.

"He loved you, you know that, right?"

"I don't. He left me on Earth, lied to me all my life. How could he have loved me? I don't even know if he ever loved my mother because he cheated on her. How could he have?" I ramble out.

"I can only tell you one thing. When we first met, when you and your father were attacked, I knew he loved you. His reactions to everything happening in those moments, were to protect you. I ran and told you to duck, only because your father was running towards you, and I knew he wouldn't make it. He was going to run straight into that dagger, no matter if it killed him, in order to save you. Whatever mistakes your father made, I believe he loved you very much," he tells me, and I smile to myself as we take a right, away from the sounds of the people and the campfire in the distance.

"I didn't know he did that. Maybe you're right," I concede quietly as I start to hear the sound of the sea and waves.

"I'm always right, kitty cat. Haven't you learnt that by now?" Dagan teases.

"You're always lacking modesty, but I don't know about anything else," I laugh, and he tickles my side, making me jump away from him as we start to see some lights.

"Where are we?" I ask as Dagan holds a branch out of the way, and I step through, straight onto a beach. We are on the rocks that lead to the water, which have several glowing white stones littered around.

"What is this place? What are those stones?" I ask Dagan as I walk over, stopping in the sand, just before the waves can reach my boots.

"Glow Stone Beach. A nice simple name, and in about ten minutes, something amazing happens. So, let's get in," Dagan explains, and I turn around just in time to see him pull his shirt off slowly and drop it on the rocks where he has already taken his cloak off. The moonlight shines on his chest, where his chiselled chest leads to a defined set of abs and distinct v shape dips into his jeans.

"Kitty cat, do you not want to swim?" Dagan asks, his voice full of amusement, and my eyes flash up to his, seeing the playfulness there. I clear my throat.

"Yep, I want to swim. But you are getting in first," I say, crossing my arms, and he laughs loudly. He kicks his boots off, pulling his socks off next, and then drops his jeans until he is completely naked, totally shameless as he stands in front of me. I don't let my eyes drop from his, which only seems to amuse him more as he walks past me, straight into the water. *Holy crap, he is going to kill me with his hotness. If that's even possible.*

"Hurry up, kitty cat," Dagan says, snapping me out of my thoughts. I quickly strip down, leaving my clothes piled next to Dagan's before running into the warm water. I swim out to the nearest glowing rock, grabbing it as I place my hands against it, feeling how warm the stone is.

"Boo," Dagan says next to my ear, his hands slipping around my waist. I relax my head back on his shoulder as we float in the waves quietly for a while.

"Turn around, it should be any second," Dagan whispers and helps me turn in the water. I rest my arms around his shoulders, looking up as he tucks a bit of my hair behind my ear.

"What's this surprise then?" I ask, feeling curious now, but I'm also a little overwhelmed by how close we are and the way he looks at me.

"This," he says, turning us sideways so I can see the millions of little blue lights in the water that are being pushed towards us by the waves. It looks like a wave of blue, sparkling diamonds, but much brighter.

"What are those? It's beautiful," I gasp in shock. This is what makes Dragca amazing.

"No one really knows. The people call them Sealights, and they come to this shore every night around this time. I've always wanted to see them," he says as the little lights surround us in the water. They don't touch us, just float around us. I wave a hand out in the water, watching how they move around my hand as I wave it in the sea.

"This is amazing, unforgettable," I mumble, still waving my hand in the sea.

"Just like you. This place reminds me of you. That's why I was so happy when I found out where we are, and I realized I could bring you here with me. This place is special, unique and so alive. It just shows, in a world where light magic is meant to be rare and practically impossible, there is this," he whispers to me. I lean closer, sliding my hand into his hair as I kiss him, and his hands tighten on my hips, pulling my body hard against his.

"I didn't bring you here for that, we can just stay and enjoy the water," he says. I almost worry he doesn't want this, but I can feel how much he wants me from where our bodies are pressed together. I drag my hand out of his hair, down his chest, and find his hard length, wrapping my hand around him.

"I want to enjoy you," I say, and he groans as I speed up with my hand.

"Isola," he rasps, pulling my hand away and gripping me tightly to him. I wrap my legs around his waist as he kisses me. Moaning when his hand grabs one of my breasts and flicks the nipple, I rock myself against his length. I slowly inch myself down on him, and he easily slips in with how turned on I am. Dagan growls as he kisses me roughly, his hands holding my hips as I move up and down, getting closer and closer to the edge.

"Mate with me?" he asks against my lips suddenly, and I stop with him still inside me. Dagan doesn't let me completely stop as he moves my hips.

"You haven't even told me you love me yet," I gasp, and he chuckles as my back hits a stone, and Dagan presses me against it, somehow pushing deeper inside me and making me moan. He glides his hand slowly up my legs as he kisses me and breaks away.

"I love you, and you know it. I know it, though I'm a damn idiot for not telling you sooner. I want you to be mine, but the choice is yours. I just thought you might want to know what I am thinking about nearly all. the. damn. time," he says, punctuating his words with kisses as he pounds harder into me.

"Yes," I moan out, and his right hand moves between us, rubbing circles on my clit as he carries on thrusting. His other hand drifts to my throat, angling my head so I have to look at him.

"Yes to what, Isola? Say the words," he taunts, not letting me go, and no part of me wants him to either.

"I will mate with you," I manage to whisper.

"Good, kitty cat. Now come for me. I want to feel you come around my cock," he growls out, and I cry out as the orgasm that was just out of reach suddenly slams through me at his words. He picks up speed, and only a few thrusts later, I feel him finish inside me as he kisses me deeply.

"Damn. I wanted to spend months getting to know you, learning everything you like, but no part of me regrets this," he mutters against my lips, and it makes me giggle.

"Good?" I ask, and he pulls back to frown at me.

"That was more than good. In fact, I think we should get out of the water, onto the sand, and see if we can do a longer repeat," he teases, sucking my bottom lip into his mouth before letting go so I can answer as he pulls out of me.

"One thing first, though," I say, pushing off the rock and wrapping my arms around his shoulders. "I love you. I needed to tell you that."

"And I needed to hear it. I won't ever forget this moment. It's the beginning of us, our future, and I'm never letting you go," he vows lovingly, and then kisses me once more.

"That's just gross. You can't drink the milk you just had a bath in, Bee," I say, watching in disgust as she shrugs at me and carries on drinking through the straw she has put in her bowl of milk. I look over the table where Thorne is quietly eating his toast, watching Bee with the same revulsion I am. He meets my eyes, and we both laugh, shaking our heads.

"Hey, sis, where are Dagan and Elias?" Melody asks, picking up the glass jug of milk and a bowl off the side before sitting at the table. Melody frowns at Bee for a second as she gets the box of chocolate cereal off the table and starts pouring some into her bowl.

"I don't know for certain about Elias, but Dagan

told me he was going to see Kor. I bet he took Eli with him," I answer, ignoring the sharp bite of pain that shoots through my heart at the thought of Eli walking out of here and not even attempting to talk to me.

"Makes sense," Melody says, pouring her milk.

"A more important question, how do they have so much human food here?" I ask, pointing at the boxes of food they gave us.

"There is a portal here that opens into the back of a supermarket in Scotland. They send a team into the portal every night there to steal a little food. The humans think there is a stock problem, and our people are fed. It's a win, win. It's part of why they chose this place, that and its close connection to the memory cave," she shrugs.

"That's kind of amazing, and what is the memory cave? You haven't told us anything about it, and I think we need to know," I say, and Thorne puts his toast down, turning so, like me, his focus is solely on Melody.

"It is where all seers go when they come of age. The cave is, in the simplest way to describe, alive with the memories of Dragca. When I went in, it showed me my mother as a child and then her being killed. It also showed me my birth and my death," she explains.

"It shows you your future?" Thorne asks.

"Yes and no. For some people, what it shows comes true, and for others it does not. Like my death, for example. I was shown that I would die protecting you in the castle when Tatarina killed the king, but that didn't happen. I wouldn't worry, the cave mostly shows you the past and helps you find where you need to go," she waves a hand.

"So, it's like your powers? They might not come true, but there is good chance they could?" I question.

"Yes, and another thing . . ." she drawls out with a slightly worried expression.

"Out with it," I say.

"The cave walls are made of the same glass as my orb. You cannot touch it, and it blocks all dragon powers," she explains.

"All we have to do is get through the cave," I say, taking a deep breath.

"You don't understand," Melody shakes her head at me as she speaks.

"Then help me," I coax her gently.

"The cave is dangerous. It will show you things

that will make you want to follow it, and then you will be lost forever. It will try to break you. Hundreds of dragons have tried to survive the cave and failed. Only one has ever survived going through it," she says.

"Who?" I ask.

"Your ancestor. The very first ice king," she says quietly and reaches for my hand on the table, covering it with her own. "If he could do this alone, then you can do this with Thorne by your side."

"It's been done before, so we can also do it," Thorne declares firmly, and when I look over at him, I don't see any fear. Just pure determination. I have to do this for them. I have to give them their dragons back, or I will never be able to live with myself. I sharply nod at Thorne, letting go of Melody's hand and standing up.

"Bee, are you ready to go train?" I ask her, and she sighs, flying up and landing on my shoulder.

"Sure. Must walk north," she says, her voice full of attitude. I raise one eyebrow at her, and she just crosses her arms.

"I am coming with you. You shouldn't be alone," Thorne says, standing up and stretching before taking his plate to the sink. I spot the quiver of arrows on his back, a sword underneath it and the bow resting on the table. It makes me think back to the time he helped me use my dragon eyes to shoot an arrow, how I hugged him like he was my best friend, and how I felt something more than friendship in that moment. It's hard not to think of our past with a tinted vision now I know he was deceiving me, plotting to betray me the whole time. I turn around, walking out the door and into the living room. I pick up my cloak off the sofa, pulling it over me and tucking it underneath Bee on my shoulder before clipping it. I wait by the front door until Thorne comes out with a bag on his back as well as his weapons.

"I can carry the bag, all of that has to be heavy," I say as we walk out, and he shuts the door behind him before answering.

"No, I've got it," he replies with a smile and looks at Bee.

"Where to then?" he asks her, and I look up as she points to my right, where there isn't a path but just endless forest.

"To there," she says, looking at us like we should know the way.

"That's not a lot of information to go on Bee. We don't have time to be messing around. Why can't we train here where we know it is safe?" I ask.

"Trust?" she asks, shrugging and not blinking as

her green eyes watch me closely. It's like she is testing me in a way; I can see it in her expression and feel it deep down inside of me. I nod, looking back at Thorne who doesn't say a word, simply following me as we walk into the woods.

SEVENTEEN

"Bee, are we near yet? It's been ages," I ask her, not wanting to walk much further. We have been climbing over rocks and up hills, for the last god knows how long since we ventured into the forest. I look up, seeing the sun is right in the middle of the sky, so it must be midday already. I finish the energy bar I was eating, tucking the wrapper in my pocket as I wait for Bee to say something. "Bee, come on."

"Nearly," she responds finally, smiling at me as she sits on my shoulder. Her green hair is so long it covers her body now, and her green eyes look so innocent when she smiles at me. Like she hasn't just made me walk for miles with no explanation. *It's like all that pointless running all over again.*

"Bee, I'm worried we won't be able to get back to camp before dark if we keep walking before we even get to training," I say, and she huffs, flying off my shoulder and floating in the air in front of me, with her back facing us.

"You've pissed her off now," Thorne jokes quietly, and I laugh a little as I step up to Bee's side to see what she is seeing. There are four rocks on the mountain side, each one at least three times my size, and they are covered in dark purple vines that look like weeds. They stretch over the rock, killing the grass that is now yellow, and the flowers are all wilted.

"What is that?" I ask in shock, looking over at Thorne who seems just as confused as I am.

"Dark. Too much dark in Dragca, not enough light. No balance," Bee says, like her random statement should explain everything. Thorne walks closer, lifting his sword off his back.

"Don't get too close, be careful," I warn him, and he glances back at me with a grin.

"Didn't know you cared, Issy," Thorne says, and I roll my eyes at him before he turns back. Thorne slowly lifts his sword, touching one of the veins with its tip and a black flash of light sends him flying across the rocks.

"Thorne!" I scream, running over to him as he lands and rolls on the ground a few times. I fall to my knees next to him and turn him over onto his back. He coughs a few times before opening his eyes, and I breathe out a sigh of relief.

"Fuck, that hurt," he coughs, sitting up with my help.

"You okay?" I ask.

"Yeah," he says, managing to smile at me, but he still doesn't look great. "I might have cracked a rib, but my limited dragon healing will sort it out soon. I just need to rest for a bit to heal," he explains. I help him pull his bow and bag off his back before he leans back on the rock. I still don't move for a while, worrying that he might be more hurt than he is admitting to me.

"Go and learn, just don't touch it," he insists, studying my expression.

"Are you sure you are okay?" I ask, needing to hear him say it.

"I'm good, now go, Issy. We need you to learn whatever the hell Bee has brought you here for in order to survive that cave," he says, reaching for my hand. I don't move as he carefully pulls my hand to his mouth, kissing the back once before letting go as my heart pounds in my chest at every little movement. I'm sure when he stares into my eyes for a second, he can read my every emotion and hear my heart pounding, but luckily for me, he doesn't call me out on it.

"I should go," I say nervously, stepping back and practically running over to Bee, who is sitting on a normal rock near the weird ones. *Dark covered ones? Rocks I don't want to touch? Who knows what their name should be.*

"Bee, I think it's time you explain," I tell her, and she sits up, crossing her legs and pointing at the rocks.

"Light can destroy dark. You must find it and use," she says, moving her hand to her heart, pointing at it with her little green finger. "Feel the light, call it." I try not to laugh at the fact she sounds like someone out of Star Wars.

"That doesn't sound so easy," I say, and she laughs, floating up in the air and holding her hand out for me.

"Together now, but you can do this alone," she says, and I reach a hand out, letting her wrap her own hand around my little finger.

"What now?" I ask.

"Connect. Feel," she instructs and closes her eyes. I watch as her whole body starts to glow white before the white glow travels to her hand and touches me. I close my eyes in awe, a gasp leaving my lips. It feels like someone just threw cold water over every part of my body, and then it disappears, leaving only a weightless feeling.

"See, connect," I hear Bee say, feeling like she is all around me as I open my eyes. I smile as I see we are floating above the ground, and when I move my other hand, I notice all my skin is glowing white. I glance over at Thorne, who is sitting up watching with wide eyes, and I smile at him in reassurance. I can see something in his chest, like a yellow light.

"What is the yellow in Thorne's chest?" I ask.

"His soul. Babies are born with a white, pure soul. The soul can be tainted, and you can see the taint in time. Yellow is close to white, because Thorne is not tainted by the dark too much," Bee explains, her voice like a sweet echo, and I'm surprised how well she has learnt to speak. I look away from Bee and towards the rocks, seeing them glow with almost a black light that covers it.

"Destroy," Bee urges, letting me go, but the power never leaves me as I feel my feet graze across the floor before I land. I don't look away from the rocks as I walk over, knowing that I am meant to help them. *Help the land. Help destroy the darkness.* All these thoughts run through my head as I place my hand against the rock and a sharp pain shoots up my arm, like an electric shock. The shock buzzes through me as my hand warms up, and a bright light flows out of my hand until I can't see anything other than light.

"Isola! Enough! Stop!" I hear Thorne shout, but I ignore anything other than the need to stop the darkness, and only when I feel nothing but light, does everything fade away.

EIGHTEEN

"Any change?" Dagan asks, stepping into the small bedroom and closing the door behind him. I look back over at Isola as she lies in the bed, her eyes closed, and her skin still lightly glowing white. Her blonde hair surrounds her on the pillow, and her pink lips are the only other colour to her pale face. I think back to seeing Thorne running across the woods, holding her in his arms as she glowed like a flashlight, and Bee following not far behind them. I don't think I've ever been as scared as I was in that moment. It reminded me of the time Isola was stabbed and how helpless I felt. *And I didn't even love her back then.*

"Same as the last *six days*," I growl out, standing up from the chair and walking to the window. I stare

157

at the morning suns, just as they peek out of the tree line and slowly rise into the sky. Bird fly past, the trees sway in the breeze, and everything seems so peaceful, all while I feel nothing but panic inside of me.

"Bee said she will be fine. Try not to worry, brother," Dagan reassures me, and I glance over at him. His face is tired and tense as he strokes Isola's cheek with the back of his hand, steady rolling his lip ring around in his lips. I'm not the only one worrying and not sure if Bee is right. Bee is young, and she's not even a dragon. *What if she doesn't have a clue what she is doing?*

"The last thing I said to Isola is that I didn't want to mate with her," I lament, keeping my voice quiet as I look back at Isola, running my eyes over her beautiful face. "She doesn't even know how much I regret being a coward, or how I love her enough to be anything she wants or needs."

"Why did you tell her no?" Dagan asks as he steps back from Isola, his voice free of judgement, and it shocks me a little. I fully expected he would beat the shit out of me for hurting her because I'm an idiot.

"I'm–no, we–are children of a woman who worked at a whorehouse, and we did a lot of bad shit to just survive. I've killed so many that I don't even remember them all, and I can't make myself regret the life I've lived. What kind of mate would I make for a queen?" I say, turning away and facing the window as I clench my fists. *Who in their right mind would want me as a mate with my past?*

"A fierce mate, a mate any queen would be damn proud to have," Isola's sweet voice says, and I turn abruptly to her as she sits up, staring at me with tears on her cheeks. Her blue eyes look like they can see straight through me, like they always have done. There has been no one like her in my entire life, no one who can know me with one look like she does.

"Isola," I whisper, feeling like my feet are glued to the floor as we just stare at each other. I hear the sound of Dagan walking out of the room and closing the door behind him, but neither of us move an inch.

"No one is perfect, especially not me or my family, who have been the kings and queens, princesses and princes for thousands of years. I don't care what anyone else thinks, and I hope you don't either, because in my eyes, Elias, you are everything. Please don't think I judge you, please don't think I ever will," she whispers, and my feet finally move as I walk to the bed and fall to my knees next to her. She leans over, placing her soft hands on my cheeks, and slowly kissing me. I groan at her taste, at the feel of her, until I have to pull away.

"I don't want to fuck this all up. I've never been scared of anything as much as the thought of losing you scares me. I've always believed I was strong, brave and not a coward, until the second I hurt you the other day. I never wanted to do that, and I was a fucking idiot," I admit, and she shakes her head.

"I get it, the fear anyway. I remember when you told me once not to fall in love, because if I did, I would lose them in the end. You were right. I'm dangerous to love, and that won't change anytime soon. I get it if you want to walk out this room and never look back," she chuckles humourlessly. "Most would."

"I'm not most, naughty princess. I'm here fighting for you . . . if you will still have me?" I ask resolutely, knowing I made my mind up the second I saw the pain in her eyes from my stupid words the other day. I love her, and even if loving her is dangerous, every moment is worth it.

"I love you, but please don't hurt me again. If we keep hurting each other, there won't be anything left of us that is worth fighting for," she says, taking a deep breath.

"Never again," I say and slam my lips onto hers

in a harsh, brief kiss before I break away and keep her beautiful blue eyes locked on mine. "Mate with me, Isola Dragice? I can't offer you anything other than myself and my heart, but I will be yours forever. I will always love and protect you," I say, and she smiles widely, her eyes drifting to silver as she speaks to her dragon. I watch silently until her eyes turn back to blue.

"Yes, even my dragon agrees ... but says she will ice your feet to the floor for a week if you hurt us again," she says, and I laugh, pulling her to me. I hear the door open behind us, and Korbin walks in with Bee on his shoulder.

"Light is awake," Bee says, and Isola pulls away from me, confusion rolling over her face as she looks at me and asks one question.

"What happened?"

"Made light," Bee answers my question, flying into the room and sitting on my lap. I look away from Elias to Korbin leaning against the door frame. Kor has a leather dragon guard uniform on like the others, and I wonder who made them it for only a second as I see how well Kor looks. His tanned skin looks healthy, and his green eyes are blazing with mischief and love as he watches me.

"You're here and looking good," I say and he grins, walking over.

"Thanks, doll. You don't look too bad yourself," he jokes and places a tender kiss on my forehead.

"So, guys, how did I get from the woods to here? Everything is a little blank," I admit, looking between Kor and Eli, as they both sit on the edge of the bed. Eli puts his hand on my leg, comforting me.

Fly soon. Need mates with us, my dragon hisses in my mind.

Do you know what happened? I ask her, and all I get in return is a yawn as she ignores me, and I focus back on Eli and Kor.

"I can answer that, if I can come in?" Thorne asks from the doorway.

"Come in," I say with a smile, waving him in. Eli and Kor tense but don't openly say anything as he walks in. Thorne sits on a chair in the room, clearing his throat before talking.

"You glowed like a flashlight, and then you touched the rocks. You lit up like nothing else; I couldn't see you, I couldn't see anything but light. I tried shouting, telling you to stop," he explains, and I have a vague memory of Thorne shouting.

"I heard you, but I just couldn't stop," I say, "or I didn't want to. The power was addictive."

"What happened next?" Kor asks, sliding his hand into mine on the bed.

"The light just suddenly cut off and Isola was lying on a rock, still glowing but passed out. Bee was watching her and clapping her little hands," Thorne tells us. "Bee seemed really proud of you and told me

I didn't have to worry about you not waking up." I stare at Bee who just shrugs, her cheeks a bright-red colour.

"I'm sorry, that must have scared you," I say, looking at Thorne, but he only stares out of the window.

"I knew you weren't dead, our blood bond told me as much as I ran to you. Isola," he pauses, looking back, "the dark-purple things that covered the rocks were gone, and the rocks were covered in bright flowers and vibrant grass. You had brought the entire place back to life."

"Light can heal, right, Bee?" I ask her, and she nods, landing on my open hand.

"You are strong," she says and looks at the door.

"Food is ready," I hear Melody shout, and Bee doesn't hesitate as she flies off my hand and out of the door. *I swear Bee loves food more than anything else. I can't say I blame her.*

"How long was I sleeping?" I ask everyone.

"Six days, doll," Korbin answers, and it suddenly dawns on me.

"The trial, it's tonight, isn't it?" I ask, and Eli nods.

"You don't have to do it, you know that right?

We can live without our dragons as long as you are alive," he says, squeezing my leg.

"I need to do this. If I don't, I wouldn't be able to live with myself," I say, making sure to catch each of their eyes.

"You could die," Kor whispers hoarsely, reaching over and pushing a strand of hair behind my ear.

"The dragon guard needs to be free of this curse. Not only so you can get your dragons back, but so Tatarina doesn't have an army who can't think or act for themselves. Once the curse is broken, the dragons could leave, and the fight for the throne would not be as great," I explain. "Plus, it will earn the seers' respect and, hopefully, their help."

"We are meant to meet Essna in half an hour to start the trial," Thorne states, standing up. "Isola needs to shower and get ready."

"Are you saying I smell?" I ask, and he smirks, shrugging his shoulders once.

"Maybe," he says.

"Cheeky bastard," I mutter as he walks out, and all the guys laugh. It takes me by surprise a little at how relaxed they are around Thorne now; how I am, too.

"Thorne has a point, and I want to get your weapons ready before you go," Eli says, kissing my cheek before walking out of the room as Kor stands up.

"These are your new clothes," Kor says, picking up the pile of clothes next to him on the end of the bed and passing them to me. I smooth my hands over the supple, light-blue leather, never having seen anything like this leather before. There are even snowflakes etched into the design and a long dark-blue cloak rests under it.

"Where did this come from?" I ask Kor, still rubbing my fingers over the material.

"Bee. She made it for you while you slept," he says and points at his own clothes. "She made these, too. We all have new clothes."

"Wow," I say, speechless and amazed how she has become strong enough to make this.

"I will get some food ready for you, and the shower is through there," Kor says, going to step off the bed, but I catch his hand, stopping him.

"I love you," I whisper, and he turns our hands over, kissing the back of mine sweetly.

"I love you more," he says and lets my hand go, walking out of the room and shutting the door behind him. I slide off the bed, walking straight to the other door in the room, and catch a glimpse of myself in the full-length mirror in the bedroom just before I open the bathroom door. My whole body is slightly glowing white, my eyes look brighter, and I feel so much stronger than I was. *Let's hope I'm strong enough to survive this trial, because nothing else matters now.*

"Isola Dragice, looking every bit like the princess you are," Essna says as I walk into the clearing where she sits on her makeshift throne. Her calculating eyes watch my every step, only briefly glancing at my guards at my side, until I'm right in front of her. She has a long cloak on, her black hair is up in a tight bun, and her sharp eyes are decorated with black makeup which matches the black seer marks on her face. The marks make me think of Melody, knowing my sister has my back if Essna tries to attack me.

"Where is your sister and the light spirit?" Essna asks first, folding her hands together.

"Safe," I answer simply, and her teeth grind together, the only sign of her annoyance as she keeps her face blank. I know she wants my sister dead and to have Bee near her in case I die in that cave, but that isn't happening. Now that we know light magic isn't going to help me in the cave unless I need to heal plants, we all agreed that sending Melody and Bee to hide was the best plan. If anything happens to me, Bee will bond with Melody and that is the best option we have. *Not that I plan on dying any time soon.*

"Let's go then, we do not have time for talking. The blue moon will be upon us soon, and we must be at the entrance in time," Essna says, rising up and walking around her throne, with her seer guards following just behind her. Ten more guards surround us as we start to follow her through the crowds of people and when I look back, the crowd is walking behind us at a little distance, all whispering amongst themselves.

Safe? my dragon hisses in my mind, but I don't have a response for her. I don't think we will ever be truly safe for a long time. Essna slows down a little, falling back to walk at my side after Dagan steps away when I nod at him to say it's okay. I still feel Eli and Kor step closer, and glance over to see Thorne has his hand on his sword, watching Essna closely.

"Tell me, princess, what are your plans for

Dragca if you reclaim the throne?" Essna asks, never looking my way once as she speaks.

"I want peace, something Dragca hasn't known since my mother was alive," I say determinedly, and she laughs.

"There was never peace for the poor, for the hunted, or those who didn't want the dragon guard curse and paid the ultimate price. There was peace for the rich, but that is it, and I know that well," she chuckles, and there is a silence between us as I think about her words. *Was there ever peace when half the dragons were slaves to a curse?*

"How did you know there was never peace? It is true I only had my view from the rich side, but they seemed happy," I ask, curious.

"I was only ten when my family was killed in a fire that destroyed my village. The fire was caused by an accident, but no ice dragon came to put it out when they could have easily done so," she sighs. "I was the only survivor, and for years I travelled around Dragca, looking for food and, well, a home."

"I am sorry that happened to you," I say, though I'm still confused about why she's telling me about her past.

"Most are, but being sorry does nothing for my past or for your future. When I turned eighteen, I found this place, secretly run by Melody's mother. I was her second in command before she died," Essna explains. "I respected and loved her dearly, even with her mistake of loving your father."

"Does Melody know this?" I ask quietly. Melody seems to hate Essna, maybe she wouldn't if she knew how close her mum was to her and how her mother trusted her enough to place her as her second in command.

"Melody does not want to ask the questions she is scared of the answer to. I may be strict with her, but only because when I am gone, Melody is the rightful leader. She is too young, too strong-willed to lead the seers at the moment, but I see so much of her mother in her," Essna says, and for a moment, I think I may understand her a little better. Sometimes you can't act how you wish to in order to get the right outcome.

"When I am queen, I will change what my father always should have done. I know my words feel like an empty promise, but I can only offer you words for now. Dragca needs to unite and fight for itself, rather than being at war like it always has done," I say, looking up at the sky and enjoying the warm sunlight that streams onto my skin. It reminds me of the light and for a second, I call the light and feel it spread over me like a wash of cold water. I glance at my hand, seeing I'm glowing a little brighter than usual, but you can't tell in the bright sunlight. Essna keeps her eyes forward as I stare at her, seeing the yellow light of her soul and knowing she isn't tainted. I glance back at Kor, Elias, and Dagan, seeing they all have normal souls too, even if Elias's is the darkest yellow out of them all. The power slowly leaves me as I turn back to Essna, and she finally replies to me.

"I see you bringing change, but I also see you bringing about our destruction because of who you love," Essna says, placing her hand on my shoulder briefly, before walking ahead. "I only hope it is peace you love more."

TWENTY-ONE

"This must be it," Dagan says, and I follow his gaze to the small cavern at the bottom of a mountain we are approaching. The mountain is well-hidden in the forest, and I doubt you could see it unless you flew over it. The cavern has a massive door, with what looks like dozens of etched dragons flying around in a circle on it. The dragons are painted red, blue, black and white, which sends goose bumps all over my skin as I look at them. My eyes travel all over it, to the middle where in the center of the dragon circle is a circular hole that looks like something fits in it. There are dozens of lit candles on the ground near the mountain, many looking old and some newer. Essna walks back to me, stopping at my side with

G. BAILEY

Thorne moving to her other side. We wait for the other people following us to catch up and gather around us. Some of them carry new candles over to the other candles, lighting them and bowing their heads as they whisper.

"Seers have a tradition, every time we lose someone, every time a new seer is born, every time there is a blessed mating, we leave a candle outside here. Our tradition says the memory cave is where the first seer was born and gifted her sight. Therefore, we have always respected this place," Essna explains from my side as we come to a stop.

"Come Isola, Thorne, it is time," Essna says as the crowd parts around us, and she walks over to stand by the door. Dagan skims his hand over my face, making me turn to him, and he kisses me lightly. His blue eyes look darker than usual, with worry, I expect. I place my hand on his cheek, and he leans into it, closing his eyes for a second.

"Good luck, and come back to me, kitty cat," he whispers, stepping back as my hand falls away. Kor and Eli both kiss me goodbye next, neither one of them needing to say a word that hasn't already been said. I know they are worried, so am I, but this has to be done.

"Stay safe," I tell them all, knowing there is

nothing else I need to say. They know how I feel and that I will fight to survive this for them. *And for myself.* In nearly every romance book I've read, the main girl always wants to live for her guy, when she should want to live for herself, too. She is just as important. *I miss reading, why are there no books here, or any time for reading?*

"We will wait for you here. None of us are leaving until you return," Elias states, making me smile as I walk over to Essna. I glance back to see Elias's hand on Thorne's shoulder, whispering something to him before letting him go, so he can catch up with me. I slide my hands over the two daggers on my hips, feeling the soft material of the new leather dragon outfit, and keep my head up high as I stop near Essna. Essna pulls a flat, glass, circle-shaped object from inside of her cloak, and turns around, walking to the door. We follow her over, standing a few feet behind her as she places the object into the gap in the circle. Nothing happens for a long time, and I glance at Thorne, who shrugs in confusion. I'm about to say something when Essna steps aside, placing her hands high in the air. She looks up at the sky behind us, and I follow her gaze. The moons slowly appear out of the tree line, rising in the late evening sky as the blue light shines through the trees. Both of the moons are a bright blue colour, shining so brightly that it could be mistaken for daylight. When the moons are high enough, the light shines on the door, and we hear a clicking noise. Each one of the etched dragons lights up blue, and then the door opens itself gradually.

"Go, and good luck, princess," Essna says, and Thorne walks in first, not hesitating at all. I slowly follow him in, looking back only once as Essna closes the door and her words follow us through, echoing in the cave. "Beware of the past, because it is just that."

"HERE," Thorne says as he clicks a flashlight on and hands one to me, before clicking his own one on. Thank god he thought ahead and has a bag full of useful things.

"Thanks," I say, flashing the light around the room. It looks just like a normal cave with brown dirt, rock walls, and what I'm sure is a rat that runs past our feet. *Gross.*

"We should be careful not to touch any crystal in here," Thorne says and starts walking down the silent cave. "The burns aren't bad, but I don't fancy risking it."

"Thanks for coming with me. You didn't have to do this," I say, and Thorne chuckles as we walk quietly.

"I *did* have to do this, and not only just for you. Since I met you, I've repeatedly dreamt of walking through a cave. The same dream all the time, and something urged me to come with you. Call it what you will, but I believe fate wanted me here," he says, pushing his messy blond hair out of his eyes. He hasn't cut it in a long time, and it's long enough that the ends are starting to curl.

"Do you believe in fate? That some things are meant to be?" I ask.

"Yes. Though, I believed in it more the day I met you," he says, glancing back at me once as my heart pounds in my chest, and I look away. I don't look back as we continue walking in silence, my own thoughts not straying far from Thorne and what he means to me. The more time I spend with him, the harder it is to deny there is something between us, but it still hurts when I think of how he betrayed me. It's an an odd mixture of pain and possible love, and I know it could destroy me if I'm not careful.

"Stop," Thorne says suddenly as I walk into his

outstretched arm, which he uses to hold me back as he shines a light on the massive room right in front of us. The floor, walls, everything is smooth crystal, looking almost like a mirror.

"Mother?" Thorne says suddenly, dropping his arm and running into the room. I dash into the room after him, grabbing Thorne's hand, and a shock vibrates through my arm. I turn to where Thorne is looking and see two girls running through a woods in the glass. The image is so clear that it's like we are in a cinema or something.

"Mum?" I whisper.

TWENTY-TWO

The two girls run through the forest as we watch, holding hands and laughing loudly, glancing back every so often with big smiles on their faces. They must only be ten or so, but the one on the right is clearly my mother as a child. I've seen paintings of her in the castle, her long blonde hair and blue eyes are so much like mine that I would recognise her anywhere. The girl next to her I don't know, but she is an ice dragon, too, with short blonde hair and blue eyes, too, but hers are darker and her features sharper. The girls both have blue dresses on that sway in the wind and knock against the flowers on the ground.

"Let's stop, Tata. He won't be able to find us, we

ran too quickly," my mother giggles, dramatically throwing her arms in the air.

"Okay," Tata shrugs, lying down on the grass, and my mother lies next to her.

"Is that your mother?" I ask Thorne, sliding my hand into his without noticing I'm even doing it. I turn to him, his expression full of sadness as he watches our mothers. Everything must be clicking into place for him, everything that his mother has lied about. I look back at Tatarina, wondering how this little, innocent girl became the monster we all know now.

"Yes," he whispers back, just before my mum and Tatarina start talking.

"Everyone is saying that one of us will have to marry Ofen and become queen," Tatarina says, staring at the sky. She speaks of my father, and it hurts me to even think of him right now.

"I don't want to be queen, or marry a stinky boy, even if he *is* a prince," mum replies, and it makes me laugh as well as Tatarina.

"Nope, me neither. Boys suck, and I love you anyway," she says so innocently that I want to believe she is lying, when it's likely she isn't.

"I love you, too. You're better than anyone else,"

my mum says, and then they fade away. There is just a crystal mirror left behind, reflecting the image of me and Thorne. We stare at each other's reflection for a while, neither one of us breaking the growing tension with words. My heart breaks for him. I know what it is like to have the image of your parents smashed to pieces by finding out what they were really like.

"Our parents were friends . . . what Darth said was true. It's all true," Thorne says in shock, shaking his head and stepping away from me as he unlinks our hands. "My mother lied."

"Melody showed me a vision of your mother, a vision that showed me Tatarina had convinced your adoptive parents to kill the queen. It was all her. You might as well know all the entire truth. Somehow, they went from best friends to Tatarina wanting my mum dead and making sure she got her wish," I say, knowing he needs to know this. He needs to know who his mother really is. Thorne doesn't look at me as I go to him, placing my hand on his tense shoulder.

"No!" Thorne shouts, rubbing his hands through his hair. He jerks away from me, refusing to look my way.

"I think she did all of this because she wanted to be queen. She wanted to rule. Your mother killed mine and then married my father," I whisper. "We have all tried to tell you any parts of her that were good are gone, but I think you can finally see it now."

"Why?" Thorne shouts, walking to the crystal wall and kicking it. "Show me why!" I gasp as he slams his hands against the wall, and it burns his skin, but he doesn't stop.

"Thorne, stop!" I shout, running over and grabbing his arm to stop him, just as the crystal wall blurs again, and an image eventually comes into view. We step back together, watching as two people appear, and it becomes apparent they are Tatarina and my father, only much younger. They look like teenagers.

"It's not you, Tatarina. I'm sorry, but I love her," my father exclaims, pushing away Tatarina's arms as she tries to cling to him. She is a mess, tear-stained cheeks, messy hair, and desperate eyes that watch my father. He looks worried, but no other emotion is on his pale face. My father smooths his hair down, straightening his cloak as he watches Tatarina fall to pieces.

"We slept together just last week! You told me you loved me and wanted *me* as your queen," Tatarina pleads, and tears stream down my face as I witness her heartbreak. My father pushes her away, and she falls to the floor. My father's face is cold as he walks to the door, pausing with his hand on the handle.

"It was a mistake, and I am sorry I hurt you, but I love her," he says, and Tatarina bursts into tears as my father walks out the door. We both silently watch Tatarina break down, pulling her beautiful blonde hair out in chunks and screaming on the floor. She does eventually get up, walk past us and out of the door. The image in the wall follows her down the corridor of the royal castle, through a little door that leads to the gardens. Tatarina stops as we all see my father down on one knee, offering my mother a ring. Proposing to my mother just after he destroyed Tatarina.

"Yes! Of course I will! I love you!" my mother's sweet voice sings, and she laughs as my father picks her up and swings her around in joy. The last thing we see is Tatarina's heartbroken, tear-filled face as she walks away, and the wall turns back to the crystal mirror. Thorne falls to his knees, his head bowed. I kneel next to him, putting my hands on his shoulders and resting my head against his. I pull his hands up, going to call my ice to sooth them when I notice I can't do that. I can't feel my dragon or her emotions in here, it's like she is locked inside my head by the magic in this place.

"My whole life, even before I was born, she has lied and destroyed everything good around her, out of nothing but pure jealousy," Thorne whispers, the anguish in his voice painful to hear.

"Life is cruel at times, and it has different effects on us all. When I saw that, I only felt anger towards my father, sorrow for your mother, and sadness for my mum," I admit. No one other than my father won in that situation. Both of our mothers were hurt, because I doubt my mother knew her soon to be husband had slept with her best friend.

"All I felt was anger at my mother," Thorne says, lifting his head and locking his eyes on mine.

"Your mother killed mine, or at least made the order, and I hate her for that. I always will, but I understand her better now. She was lost from that moment we just saw, but I'm sure there is some part of her that still loves you. You are her son," I say gently.

"She doesn't love me. I was just a way for her to get the rebellion on her side," he whispers.

"You don't know that," I reply, and he laughs.

"I do. It's always meant to be like this for me. The people I love, they don't feel the same way. I might as well finally start accepting it," he says, pulling away from me and standing up. He clicks his flashlight on as I stand, and I place my hand on his shoulder.

"You don't know what she, or anyone else, feels for you," I say, and he looks down at me for a second, something shining in his eyes that I can't understand.

"Then tell me," he pleads, dropping the flashlight and grabbing my face with his hands. I don't—no can't—say anything for a while as I just relax at his touch.

"I can't say it yet. I'm not ready to admit it, but I will say that you are wrong. You are so wrong about how I feel for you," I whisper. "And you might be wrong about your mother. It's hard not to care for you, even when someone doesn't want to, or isn't ready."

"Then I will say it, and I can only hope that you do feel the same and are willing to forgive me one day. I get that I still have a lot of making up to do, and you can hate me forever if you want, but I do love you. I loved you from the first moment I saw you, and it killed me to betray you for my mother. I was torn between two women, and not knowing which side to choose. I really did believe my mother was still good, and she was doing the right thing. I wish I realised how lost my mother was, but I didn't, and I can't change the past no matter how much I wish I could," he says, and I lean up, brushing my lips against his ever so gently before pulling away before it can become a real kiss, and I'm honestly surprised that he lets me.

"You're right. I can't just forgive and forget, but I can't let you go either. This is so complicated between us, but I'm not denying there is something more here than just our past. There was something from the moment we met, and together we can build again," I assure him, and he pulls me to him, holding me close.

"Thank you. I promise I will never let you down again. Never," he says into my hair, kissing the top of my head.

"You best not," I chuckle, wishing I could hear my dragon's thoughts on the matter, but she is still locked away from the magic in here. I don't even want to know Eli's, Kor's, and Dagan's thoughts on this when we get out of here. They are likely going to flip a lid, but I won't lie to them.

"We should get going. We need to get out of here," I say, pulling away but keeping my hand linked with his. He carefully picks up the flashlight from the floor without touching the crystal. Thorne flashes the light around the cave, and we both see the cave we came through is gone, and there is just a wall in its place now. There is another tunnel on the other side, and I guess that's the only way we can go.

"Are your hands okay?" I ask, feeling a little bit of the burns on his knuckles with my hand as we walk towards the tunnel and step off the crystal.

"Yeah, they don't hurt much," he shrugs, but I bet they do. *Men and their egos.*

"What is that?" I ask, seeing a light at the end of the tunnel just ahead of us.

"Maybe it's the exit?" Thorne asks.

"I don't think so . . . That would make it too easy . . ." my voice trails off as we walk into the light, and I take in the sight in front of me. The clearing is a meadow with white, glowing grass and five black trees in the middle of the grass. There are white flowers which smell amazing as we walk closer to the trees, and everything suddenly starts to feel a little hazy.

"Thorne . . ." I manage to whisper as his hand lets go of mine, and he falls to the floor. My legs can't seem to hold themselves up as I drop right next to him, seeing his lips form my name just before everything goes black.

TWENTY-THREE

"Hello?" I call, opening my eyes and staring at the empty ballroom in front of me. This room is from the castle. How did I get here? Where is Thorne? The ballroom is covered in flowers, a table full of presents is in one corner, and there's also a table full of food. I turn and look at the thrones at the front of the room. One large one, and one a little bit smaller. There are three pairs of thrones in different rooms of the castle, if I remember correctly, and I used to love watching my mother and father sitting on them, their crowns shining. They always looked so proud and happy. When nothing happens for a while, I start to panic, turning in circles. Where is Thorne?

"Thorne?" I shout, though my voice doesn't seem to make a sound around the room. The double doors *suddenly open behind me, and I turn, seeing my mother walk in, her stomach large with pregnancy, and my father right behind her. My mum looks furious as she stops in the middle of the room. My mother has a long, stunning blue dress on, that matches my father's blue shirt. All blue, all representing the ice dragons that are nearly extinct now.*

"All this time . . . all this time you never told me you slept with Tatarina? Then you cheat on me with the royal seer who is now pregnant! How many others?" my mum demands, screaming at him, and ice starts spreading across the gold floor as she shouts.

"Mum," I croak out, trying to go to her, but I can't move an inch, it's like I'm glued to the spot.

"No one else. Those were mistakes, grave mistakes," my father pleads, reaching for my mum, but she steps back.

"Liar! I know about the maid you just slept with, during our child's blessing ceremony of all things! While everyone is here to celebrate the fact that our child is nearly here, and you are too busy fucking the maid! A maid who was my friend!" mum spits out and walks over to him, slapping him hard around the face. He lets her, not moving as blood drips down his chin.

"I am sorry," he says.

"Tatarina was my best friend, and I never under-

stood why she hated me so much like she does now. You took her from me because you are a spoiled brat who thinks he can have anyone and anything he wants!" mum growls and walks around him, towards the door. "I tell you now, you will never have me again. Publicly I will be a queen for you, but that is it."

"And our child? You can't tell her, she would hate me," he pleads.

"I will tell her everything about her father and what he has done when she is old enough to understand. Now never come near me again unless it's business about the crown," she says coldly and walks out of the room, leaving my father standing, watching her go. He falls to his knees, his head in his hands, and as I watch, I just hate him.

The vision suddenly blurs, and the room spins rapidly. I have to close my eyes as I fall to my knees as everything shakes. When the shaking stops, I open my eyes and look down at the long red dress I'm wearing. The dress is massive, something a queen would wear. I stand up slowly, staring out at the ballroom, which is completely on fire now. Pieces of the ceiling fall around me as I stand still in the middle of it. So much fire.

"I always knew you would bring fire and darkness. This is your future," a cold voice says behind me, and I turn, seeing Tatarina watching me with a huge smile.

"*No,*" *I whisper.*

"*To Dragca, may it burn eternal,*" *she laughs, and everything, thankfully, fades away.*

"Isola? Isola, wake up!" Thorne's voice calls to me, but everything seems groggy as I force my eyes open and look at the cave ceiling. "Here," Thorne says, helping me up slowly and offering me some water from his bag. I drink some quickly, looking back over at the trees and meadow in the next room as I try to collect my thoughts.

"The blossom in the trees must be some kind of herb. Made to make you pass out and see visions. I saw some weird stuff, but Melody gave me an herb before we left. She said to take it when we entered the cave," he says, and I chuckle, wiping my eyes to wake myself up. "I guess it woke me up."

"Sounds like Melody. Mysterious and random," I say, my mind flashing back to the vision I saw. My father and mother hated each other, they always did. The vision of the future, of everything burning, and Tatarina winning.

"What's wrong?" Thorne asks, clearly seeing something in my expression.

"The vision showed that my father was always

cheating on my mother, that she knew and hated him for it my entire life. Then it changed, showing me a version of the future that we cannot allow to happen," I whisper.

"The vision showed me that my mother never loved my father, and she just used him to further her plan," he says, smoothing his hands down my arms and leaving goose bumps. "I think we qualify for the most fucked-up parents award, don't you?"

"Yep," I laugh.

"Our parents are not us, and we can be better than them. That's all the vision was trying to show us, that we are better than they were. That somehow, we learnt right from wrong, even if it wasn't taught to us by both our parents," he says, helping me stand up as the room still sways a little.

"My mum taught me right from wrong, and I now know she is the bravest and most selfless woman I ever met. She put me and the crown before her own happiness," I say.

"You won't ever have to do that," he insists.

"Who knows what the future will bring? Now we need to find a way out," I say, straightening up and holding onto Thorne's hand. He puts the water away, and we start walking down the path we are on. It leads through a few more rooms made of crystal until we get to a much bigger room, full of treasure.

"It looks like a pirate hid all his treasure here," I gasp, staring at the piles of gold, jewels, and various other things littered around.

"Yeah, more like ten pirates and an army of jewel thieves maybe," Thorne mutters.

"I don't think we should touch anything. On Earth, they have tales of dragons hoarding jewels and gold, that they love shiny things and will do anything to protect them. Maybe there is some truth to it?" I suggest as we walk through the piles of gold.

"Humans are smarter than they look, children of Dragca, and the rumour is very much true," an old lady's voice drifts over to us. We look over to our left, seeing an old woman sitting on a gold throne, holding an old but deadly-looking staff. She has a black, ragged cloak on that covers her body, and her long grey hair falls around her shoulders.

"We didn't come here to steal. We just want to pass through here," I say, locking my eyes with her blue ones. I don't know why, but some part of me is cautious of the woman.

"I know. Yet you want something, you just do not know what," she says, speaking in riddles.

"Can you offer me something I want?" I ask.

"For a price, yes," she says, a big smile appearing on her dry, cracked lips.

"What is the price?" I ask hesitantly. Her haunting laugh fills the room as her next words frighten me.

"A price you will never give willingly."

"Explain? What wouldn't I give?" I ask, holding my hands on my hips. The old lady laughs again, lifting her staff and pointing it at Thorne.

"Love, the throne, and most of all, your people. You care too much to be a queen," the lady says. "A trait you have from your mother. Though, I do like people who care more for others than themselves."

"What is your name?" I ask, wondering how she knew anything about my mother, but learning her name might be the best start.

"Secrets are best kept that way, don't you think?" she says, moving her eyes between me and Thorne.

"You've lost me with all these riddles. We want

to get out of this cave, not stand around talking. Let's go, Isola," Thorne says in a frustrated tone, and the old lady shoots a white light at him from the staff, making him fall to the ground with a thud.

"Thorne!" I scream, kneeling next to him and feeling his neck, thankfully finding a pulse.

"Don't you go worrying, he will be fine. I needed him out of the way, so we ladies could speak about the important things," she says, chuckling as I glare at her. "Men only get in the way, especially a sexy one like him."

"Talk about what?" I ask, standing up and staying in front of Thorne, though I cringe at her words. She suddenly loses all traces of amusement from her face.

"There must be balance, and very soon the balance will tip all the way in the favour of darkness. Now dark does not mean evil, nor does light mean good," she says, and I'm sure I have heard that somewhere before, but I can't remember where.

"Balance?" I question.

"All the worlds must have balance. We all have a choice, but none matter as much as your choice does," she says, her random sentences not making a bit of sense to me. It's like she jumps from one thought to another without explaining the last.

"Choice about what?" I ask.

"If you wish to become the balance or not," she says. "Though, you were born to be. Every time a balance is born here, they are either destroyed by the power, or they reject it. I do look forward to your choice," she says, smiling at me like she is proud of me or something.

"Lady, this isn't making much sense to me. What is the balance? What choice? What price?" I ask, shooting questions off rapidly, and she sighs deeply.

"Children," she huffs. "They have no patience at all these days."

"That doesn't exactly answer my question," I mutter as the lady carefully stands up and beckons me over. I glance once more at Thorne, who looks fast asleep and safe, before walking over to her because I know we need answers. She then walks through the piles of gold, and I follow until she stops so suddenly that I slam into her back. I collect myself before walking to her side and stare at the row of rocks in front of us. Ten rocks, all different colours and each one is floating.

"Balance is important in all worlds. Earth. Dragca, Frayan, and many others that are interlinked," she says. I know of Earth and Dragca, of course, but not Frayan.

"Frayan?" I ask.

"There are portals on Earth to it, it's where fairies are from. Did you really think you were the only supernatural being alive? I believe there is even a war on Earth as we speak, destroying one of its main cities. The one with the pointy tower," she clicks her fingers in the air as I try to process her information. "Never mind the name of the place, Earth is not important right now."

"Who the hell are you? How do you know all this?" I demand, staring at her.

"Earth people call me a goddess, others call me a fate, and I have many, many other names you will never have heard of. I travel between worlds to do my job, to keep my power," she explains.

"Fate? You are fate?" I ask.

"One of many, at your service." She grins, a toothless one at that. "That is the human saying, yes?"

"Erm, yep," I reply, completely weirded out.

"Where were we? Oh yes, balance," she snaps her fingers, and the stones shake a little.

"Are the stones the balance?" I ask.

"No. You are. The people on Dragca, the dragons,

the humans, and every being here. If darkness takes over, light will have to defend it," she says. "Dragca cannot fall, because Earth and Frayan would not be far behind. Millions, billions will die."

"You mean Bee and I have to defend it?" I ask in a hoarse whisper from the pressure her words create, and she smiles.

"Ah, the light spirit. Funny little things, aren't they? What is your dark spirit called again?" she asks, and I give her a confused look.

"I don't have a dark spirit, only a light one," I explain.

"Oh, I forgot. Silly me," she smacks her head with the staff. "I also forgot that this is for you." She hands me the staff, and I have no choice but to accept it, as she lets it fall into my open hands. I lift it up, examining the two deadly spikes on either end, and the twirls engraved all the way down it. The lady pushes a red gem right in the middle of the staff, and I step back in shock as the staff goes all bendy and snake-like as it gets smaller. It suddenly swirls around my arm, stopping with the red gem on my wrist.

"What the hell?"

"I've been to Hell, and it is not a nice place. Nasty demons there, child," the lady chuckles as I stare at my arm as I move it around.

"How does it work?" I ask, holding my arm out, and she looks at me like I'm an idiot.

"It's a royal weapon, a magic staff that can channel your ice and light powers. Only your blood line can use and wear it. The staff will change with you when you shift, and if you need to use it, you only have to push the red gemstone," she says in exasperation, like I should know all this.

"Thank you," I say honestly, knowing the staff could be very useful and very well might save my life one day.

"It belongs to your blood line, your very first ancestor made it. I would know, I was there," she laughs. "He was a funny man. I did like him very much."

"How old are you?" I ask as she continues to laugh, and she shakes her head, tapping the side of her nose to let me know I don't have a chance of getting that answer. I'm willing to bet she is pretty old.

"Now, we must discuss a price for the gift," she hums, rubbing her hands together.

"What gift?" I ask, guessing she doesn't mean the staff.

"I can tell you how to break the dragon guard

curse. It is rather easy, actually, I'm surprised no one thought of it before, but you will need my help," she chuckles.

"You know how to break it?" I ask.

"Yes. Why else would Essna send you in here? She isn't a bad girl that one," the lady winks, and then the playfulness leaves her eyes.

"What is the price?" I whisper, dreading her response. From the look she is giving me, I know I won't like it.

"The price for the answer you seek is dear. In many years, when your firstborn turns eighteen, she is to be sent to me. No one will see her for three years, and my price will be taken," she says, almost singing the words, and I feel the power connected to them.

"What will you do with her?" I ask, my voice a mere rasp.

"I cannot tell you more, only that it is her fate. You must also never tell her of the promise you make me today. She cannot know in advance," she says and places her hand on my arm. "Do not worry, I see many children in the future you seek."

"You're asking me to hand over my child to you, my firstborn, the heir of Dragca, if I win the throne?" I whisper.

"Yes. It is not an easy price to pay, but without my knowledge, you will never have a child to give me anyway," she says simply. "I cannot offer the help of a fate without a price. I do not wish to cause you more pain, Isola Dragice. I know your life has not been kind to you so far."

"Can you promise me her safety? That she will not be harmed?" I ask, needing at least that much to be answered.

"I promise that she will be under my protection. That is all I can say," she says, and steps over to the rocks. As I watch, she grabs the glowing blue one, crushing it in her hand and when she opens her hand, a long silver chain holds a tiny blue rock.

"You must wear this every day, until the time comes for you to fulfill your promise. Give it to your daughter when you bring her here in several years," she says.

"There isn't really a choice, is there? The curse must fall at the final promise. That's what the prophecy says. This is my fate, and my child will be the price and promise," I whisper and walk forward, tears streaming down my cheeks. I wrap my hand around the chain, lifting it and placing it over my head, so it falls around my neck.

"I promise," I breathe out roughly, and the stone

glows briefly before settling back down. I look back up at the lady, who is smiling widely.

"Brilliant," she claps. "Let's wake your man, well, one of them, up. We will be needing him to break the curse."

TWENTY-FIVE

"Thorne," I shake his shoulder a few times before he abruptly sits up, his hand automatically going to his sword. His eyes focus on me, and he seems to relax a little as he sees that I'm okay.

"What happened?" he asks, and I rest my hand on his that covers the sword and shake my head.

"It's okay, the lady just needed to talk to me alone," I tell him, and he looks over my head, where the old lady—well, goddess—is sitting on the gold throne again. She just smiles widely, and in a pretty creepy way, too.

"Don't do that again," he warns her, and she chuckles as I help Thorne stand up.

"I promise," she winks at me, and I roll my eyes at her playful attitude.

"What is this?" Thorne asks, first holding my arm out to look at the staff and then looking at my necklace.

"A long story, and something that can wait," I say, pleading with him to trust me. He does, nodding his head once, and he links our hands.

"How do we break the curse?" I turn and ask the lady.

"Simple. You must mate with the half ice and half fire prince. The curse was made so no dragon guard and ice dragon could ever be together. So that dragon guards could never get the throne, and no half-blood would rule. If you two are mated, the curse will break. The curse was made from a place of love, from a mate desperate to save her king. The curse was never there to stop this. Fire and ice must rule, and the curse must break," she says, muttering the end as I stare up at Thorne.

"It can't be that simple!" Thorne refutes, shaking his head.

"Love is not simple, boy, you know this," the lady says, tutting at him.

"So, any half-blood could have stopped the curse by marrying a royal?" I ask.

"Yes. There is a reason the mixing of ice and fire dragons was kept secret. Your father knew how to break the curse, but that would have risked his army. So, he sent dragon guards to kill any half-bloods, just in case, to prevent you from ever falling in love with one. Seems he didn't find them all," she says as she winks at me again.

"Wait, we never agreed to mate," I whisper, looking up at Thorne.

"I won't push you for this. I know you don't love me fully yet, and it's too soon," Thorne tells me.

"You only need to say the words, share the blood, and I can bless you both. The rest of the mating can wait. Many have been mated without love or feelings. You do not need them," she informs, and pulls out a white stone. "I happen to have your mating stone right here."

"Isn't that meant to appear to me? To us?" I ask.

"Who do you think drops them for people to find? Sounds like a job for a fate, no?" she winks at me once more. *What is with all the winking?*

"Can Isola and I have a second alone?" Thorne asks, and she nods, leaning back in her chair. We walk around a pile of gold, and Thorne starts pacing the moment we are hidden.

"Stop a minute," I say, grabbing his arm.

"I can't make you do this; you don't want this. You don't want *me*. I don't want you to mate with me out of obligation. I want you to choose this and want it, want me," he sighs, pushing my hand away, "and I can see it in your eyes that you don't."

"I do want this, Thorne. Maybe not exactly mating yet, but I'm already bound to you in a way. I hate that I want this when I should still hate you. I hate that I can't tell Dagan, Kor, or Eli before we do this. I hate that we don't have more time to get to know each other, but I don't hate *you*. If anything, it's the opposite," I say, placing my hand back on his arm, and this time, he doesn't push me away.

"Isola, you don't have to say that," he says, and I grab his other arm, making him look down at me.

"I would never mate with someone I wasn't sure I want in my life. This curse needs to be broken. Let me give you back your dragon, and we can spend the rest of our lives working on us. Even if we end up as just friends, I want you in my life, and we will always mean something to each other," I say, and he smiles.

"You sure?" he asks, tucking a piece of my hair behind my ear.

"Positive," I grin, and he kisses my forehead. I

lean in, closing my eyes, and breathe in his smoky, almost frost-like scent.

"I haven't got all day, you know!" the lady shouts, and I chuckle, linking my hand with Thorne's as we walk back over to her. She stands from the chair as we get closer, making the white mating stone float into the air above our heads when we stop.

"How are you doing that?" Thorne asks, and she laughs as she pulls a dagger out of her cloak, not answering his question.

"Thorne, why don't you start off with the ancient words? Do you know them?" the lady asks.

"I do," he says, taking my other hand in his and holding them between us as he speaks. "Link to the heart, link to the soul. I pledge my heart to you, for you, for all the time I have left. My dragon is yours, my love is yours, and everything I am, belongs with you." I repeat his words, watching as the white mating stone starts to glow, growing brighter with every sentence we speak. Our mating is blessed.

"Please hold out your hands," she requests, and we both do. She cuts Thorne's first and then mine as I hold in the pain-filled cry that threatens to escape my lips from the sting.

"Light and dark, good and evil, and everything that makes these ones dragons, please bless this mating. We bless you," the lady says, and I lock eyes with Thorne as we link hands. A blast of white light shoots out of the mating stone, sending us both flying apart. I roll as I land on top of a pile of gold, the white light making it impossible to see anything. As the light dims, my eyes widen at the sight of Thorne's dragon standing on a pile of gold. I've never seen his dragon before, and it's amazing. The wings and body are red, but covered with blue spikes that match his blue eyes.

"Isola, my dragon is back," Thorne's deep, shocked voice floats into my mind, as well as a touch of his elation I can sense. *We are mated. Holy crap. The dragon guard curse is broken.*

"I can hear you in my head," I chuckle, and I hear his laugh as his dragon snorts out ice and fire at the same time.

"None of that, I do not want my home on fire or frozen, thank you very much," the lady shouts, stamping out the fire with her foot and shaking her stick at Thorne. I slide down the pile of gold, tripping a bit, but managing to land somewhat gracefully.

"Thank you," I tell the lady as I walk over to Thorne and place my hand on the side of his head.

"Do not thank me just yet. Anyhow, you must leave," she says and points a stick up in the air to the ceiling. "That is your way out. Good luck, Queen Isola Dragice. I do look forward to the day we meet again."

"Goodbye," I say, watching as she walks through the gold, looking back at me once more.

"When you meet a woman called Queen Winter, make sure you tell her that her aunt says hello," she states cryptically, totally confusing me. Her body seems to slowly fade before she disappears altogether. I guess I will be meeting another queen. *Let's hope she is friendly.*

"Well . . . that wasn't weird at all," Thorne mutters in my head, and I nod, still looking at the space where she once was.

"I can't call my dragon in here. I have no idea how you are, now that I'm thinking about it, but I will climb up, and you can fly us out of here," I say out loud, turning and pulling myself up onto his back after he leans down.

"If you wanted to ride me, you only had to ask," he chuckles in my mind.

"Get your head out of the gutter. Besides, you need to prepare yourself. It's likely Eli and the others are going to try and kill you for mating with me once we get out of here," I laugh, hearing his own grumble in my head. I slide myself between two of the spikes on his neck and wrap my arms around the one in front of me.

"They can try, now hold on," he warns, and spreads his wings out, knocking over everything as he bats his wings and pushes down with his legs, shooting up to the top of the cave. I hold my head down as Thorne slams into the ceiling of the cave, breaking out into the night sky. He flies up into the sky, levelling himself out as I look at the stars.

"Can you see that? Something is wrong," Thorne's worried voice drifts over to me in my mind, and I lift my head, seeing the forest on fire in lots of places, seconds before I hear the screams.

Danger. I sense Tatarina, my dragon hisses.

"Dragons incoming," I shout, spotting five of them flying straight towards us, suddenly appearing out of the trees. They don't look right; their dragons are flying way too shakily, and they look almost grey. *What the hell are those?* I move myself from between the spikes and walk down Thorne's body as he tries to fly us away.

I'm going to shift in the air. We haven't done this

before, but we need to now. You ready? I ask my dragon, and she roars in my mind.

Be right back, mate, I say to Thorne, who doesn't seem to realise what I'm about to do. I run and jump right off his tail, falling and opening my arms as my dragon takes over.

TWENTY-SIX

"What the hell is wrong with them?" I shout, driving my sword into the heart of another dragon guard. I look down at him, examining his black eyes and the black veins all over his pale skin. They are almost like zombies, and they fight like them, too. The dragon guards should be more trained than this.

"Tatarina has done something to them!" Elias shouts back as he kills two of the guards in one broad swipe of his sword. I look around, seeing only a few more of the dragon guard coming for us. I'm running straight through the woods when I see a little girl screaming as she runs away from three dragon guards who are trying to kill her. She can only be eight, and they are attacking her. I catch up to the little girl and push her behind me. She's shaking and absolutely terrified.

"Stand by that tree and close your eyes," I tell her. She does as I ask with a single nod and tears streaming down her dirt-covered cheeks. I turn to face the guards, anger burning through me.

"Come on then, don't you think you should play with someone your own size, you bastards?" I shout as they run at me with their black eyes. I kick the first one, slicing my sword across his neck and swinging to meet the next guard. He slams his sword against mine as the third guard runs for the girl. From the corner of my eye, I can see where she stands, still holding onto the tree with her eyes closed.

"No!" I yell, pushing against the sword with my other hand, cutting it, and slamming the guard back. I quickly pull out a dagger from my belt and slam it into his chest, and I keep moving, running at the girl, trying to reach her before she gets hurt. Kor appears from behind the tree, throwing his sword into the guard's chest just before he can get to her, and the guard falls to the ground.

"Good timing, man," I breathe out, going back to yank my dagger out of the other guard and sliding it back into my belt. Kor kneels next to the girl, who won't open her eyes and shakes her head of red hair. I walk over, placing my hand on Kor's shoulder. He looks between us and stands up.

"I will keep an eye out," he says, standing behind me as I kneel in front of the girl.

"Hey, what is your name?" I ask gently.

"Isie," she mumbles, sobbing on her words.

"Isie, I need you to open your eyes and answer something for me," I tell her.

"Okay," she says shakily and finally looks at me. "You saved me. You are like a brave prince." I smile at her words and pull my cloak off my back, wrapping it around her shoulders.

"What happened in the seer village? We don't know anything as we were here waiting for princess Isola to come out the cave," I explain to her, spotting Elias walking over to us. She grips my cloak tightly before she answers.

"The guards came while we were all sleeping, and the woman with black stuff all over her was telling them to kill us all. The guard killed my mummy, and my father told me to run," she says, bursting into tears again. I pick her up, holding her close as I turn around, hearing the sound of footsteps.

"Someone is coming," Elias says, stepping in

front of me and the child, guarding us with Korbin. We watch the treeline anxiously as we hear people running, and a woman comes into view. She runs, holding a baby, and five other small children are with her. They all look covered in dirt and blood. *Maybe whoever did this let them go?*

"Auntie!" Isie shouts, wriggling in my arms to get down, and I let her. She runs to her aunt, who holds her close as we come over.

"What happened?" Elias demands. The woman is clearly panicked and scared, her cloak is covered in blood, and her brown hair is littered with leaves. The children all hide behind her, looking terrified.

"The queen has done something dark to all of those guards. I was in charge of the nursery for the night. We barely escaped. They don't know who we are, who they are, and have no control over who they kill," she blurts out and looks behind her before staring at us. "We have to leave. The children are not safe. You could come with us and protect us."

"We have to wait for the princess, but keep running. We won't let anyone follow you," I say firmly, and she nods.

"Good luck. If we make it, we will pray for the princess. The true heir of Dragca," she says, bowing her head, "and her mates." I nod back before she runs carefully through the forest with the children trailing close on her heels. Isie waves once before following them, clutching my cloak.

"I don't like this. Melody and Bee are in the village," Kor says, rubbing his face. "My parents are, Darth . . . we have to go back." I catch his shoulder as he starts to walk that way.

"No. Isola needs us," I remind him.

"She will never forgive us if we let Melody and Bee get killed," Elias points out, and I shake my head at them both.

"We can't–" I stop as a light bursts in the sky, a bright light like nothing else I've ever seen, and a warm feeling slams into my body, causing me to fall to my knees.

Fly, my dragon hisses in my mind, the shift taking over before I can even think or comprehend what just happened.

You're back, I say, feeling so relieved and whole. My dragon stretches out its body after the shift, and I know somehow Isola has broken the dragon guard curse. I roar, looking over at Korbin's and Elias's dragons. They seem to be in shock, just standing there, shaking their heads.

Minnnee, my dragon hisses, turning its head to the sky just as a dragon breaks out of the mountains and into the sky. I instantly recognise the blonde head of hair as Isola riding on Thorne's back through the skies.

Danger, I shout to my dragon, seeing five other dragons flying towards them. My dragon stretches its wings out just as Isola stands up and jumps straight off Thorne's back.

*F*ight, my dragon hisses in my mind as her wings spread out in the air, and she starts to fly. We turn around mid-air, feeling Thorne's dragon at my side as we face the others as they get closer. They shoot fire in the shape of spheres at us, and my dragon drops under them, shooting straight towards them.

Kill them! I demand of her, and she shoots her own spheres of ice at them in a flurry of ice and fire that Thorne shoots with me. I drop down as the dragons get too close, and Thorne does the same, but he goes above them. My dragon looks up just in time to see two of them get hit with Thorne's attack of ice, and they drop into the trees. One of the dragons slams into me while I'm not looking, digging his claws into my wings as we fall together, and I cry out in pain. I look up, seeing three more dragons flying towards Thorne as he fights two off on his own.

No! I scream in my dragon's head as we fall through the trees and land on the ground, his claws finally coming free of my wings, so I can move. I shoot ice onto his wings as he tries to fly and keep shooting it until his entire dragon is frozen to the ground. His dragon's eyes almost dead as I stare at him encased in the ice. I look up, not seeing Thorne or any other dragons flying around.

"It has been a long time, Isola, don't you think?" Tatarina's cold, dead-sounding voice says from behind me, and my dragon turns to roar at her. I feel down my wings, knowing the damage to them is too much, and I won't be able to fly out of here for a bit. There is only one thing we can do, even if it makes me vulnerable.

Let me takeover, I ask my dragon, who doesn't hesitate as we shift back. I stand up straight, keeping my head high as I face Tatarina. She stands still like a ghost; her dark, nearly brown hair blowing in the wind is the only movement. Her eyes are completely black, and they match the dark glow her skin now has. I look over as a woman steps out from the shadows of the trees, making me take a step back.

"Bu-but, I killed you!" I gasp as Esmeralda stands by her sister's side, smiling widely with her blood-red lips. Her eyes are now as red as her hair, and her pale skin is littered with black veins.

"Death was not my ending," Esmeralda replies, her voice croaking and broken in places. Her head twitches as she speaks, and Tatarina places her hand on her sister's arm.

"I will remember to chop your head off next time," I sneer. "Just to be sure."

"There will not be a next time, for this is *your* ending, Isola," Tatarina says, holding her hands out at her sides. "You are alone, and I am queen. Is this what you always thought would happen?"

"I kinda hoped I would have killed you by now, but I still have time," I say, feeling for the staff on my arm and knowing I can fight her.

"You could join me," she says simply, and I just laugh.

"The throne is mine! I am the heir, and I will claim it back when I have killed you! You killed my mother, my father, and had your sister kill Jace! There is so much death on your hands, and you do not deserve to live!" I spit out at her, and for only a brief second does she flinch at my words.

"Mother, don't do this," Thorne says from behind me, and I turn, seeing him walking to my side with Kor and Dagan next to him. Thorne and his mother stare at each other, and a flood of pain enters my body from Thorne's emotions, not that I would have expected any less.

"Where is Elias?" I hiss at Dagan as he gets to my side.

"During the fight with those other dragons, we got separated. I'm sure he will find us soon," Dagan whispers back, and I try to swallow the worry and guilt that floods me. I know he isn't dead, with our blood bond I would feel it. *So, he must be okay.*

"Do you really choose her? I'm your mother, and I can give you the throne! All I ask is that you kill her!" Tatarina gets more and more frustrated with every word, and I swear there is actually some kind of emotion coming from her.

"This isn't a choice," Thorne replies, glancing at me. "It never was. You have lost your mind, do you really want to lose your son, too? Is the throne worth it?"

"It's me or her," Tatarina growls, never taking her eyes off Thorne.

"Is that what you asked my father? I mean, when he chose my mother over you," I ask, and she growls, black ice dripping from her hands as she steps closer, focusing her attention on me instead of Thorne.

"No!" she spits out.

"It was, wasn't it? All of this because my father was an asshole and didn't choose you. You don't have to do this, you don't have to lose your son and make him choose," I say, and she laughs.

"I can smell your mating, he has already chosen," Tatarina says.

"Mating?" Dagan hisses, and I can't look away from Tatarina and Esmeralda as they step forward together to answer him.

"It's time you ran, little girl. Change is coming, and there is no room for the light on Dragca anymore," Tatarina says, and a dark spirit flies out of the trees, landing on her outstretched hand. The dark spirit looks so much like Bee, but with dark-blue skin and black hair. She is still beautiful, even if she is dark. Her dark eyes meet mine, and there's a shock that flitters through me as we stare at each other. I almost step forward, but Kor grabs my arm to stop me.

"There is always a place for light and the true

queen," Melody says, just as I feel Bee land on my shoulder. I glance over to see her stop next to Dagan, nodding at me, even as she is covered in blood, missing her cloak and holding her orb under her arm.

"Good, you are all in one place. It will make this so much easier," Tatarina says, and I see her smile widely.

"There is a portal to our left, we run," Bee whispers in my ear as I look back at Tatarina. *We need a distraction.*

"Are you really so bitter over one man turning you down that you will destroy the whole world?" I ask her, and she growls loud.

"Once I've destroyed *your* love, let me know if you feel like destroying the world in revenge," she counters and clicks her fingers. Two guards walk out, carrying an unconscious Elias who hangs between them, his hair covered in blood. I scream, going to run forward, but both Thorne and Dagan hold my arms, stopping me. I swallow the panic in my throat and force my eyes away from Elias as Tatarina smirks at me.

"No," Dagan growls out, fire feeling like it is burning my arm where he holds me, but it doesn't actually burn me. I honestly don't really notice as I stare at Tatarina's every movement. Tatarina walks over to Elias, and I clench my fists, trying to hold myself back. She lifts his head by grabbing a fistful of his hair, showing me his bruise-covered face before letting his head drop back down.

"This one is pretty, such a shame he has such bad taste in women," she says, twirling a piece of his hair around her finger.

"Let him go," I demand, my hands shaking as ice drips onto the floor, mixing with the blood on my arms from the cuts. My dragon roars in my mind, and I have to push her away to stop the shift.

"Why?" she asks, laughing deeply, still touching my Elias. I'm going to kill her for this. *Slowly.*

"You can have me if you let him and my friends go," I say, starting to panic as I spot the thirty or maybe more guards surrounding us, hiding in the trees.

"No," Kor growls, pulling me back by my arm.

"Best listen, you cannot beat me," she laughs. "But you can watch as I destroy all the light. Nane?" she asks, looking at Nane who flies towards her hand once again.

"What are you doing?" I ask, just as Nane touches her hand, and she kneels down, digging her hand into the dirt. Her whole body glows black, and thick smoke flows from her body, spreading quickly.

"This place, it's the source of all of Dragca's magic. What do you think happens when I flood it with darkness?" Tatarina asks, and my eyes widen as I realise what she is going to do.

"Stop!" Bee shouts and falls off my shoulder as Tatarina slowly destroys all the light, and I can't stop her. I catch Bee, and Melody takes her off me.

"Protect me, sister, and the light will soon be gone," Tatarina says, a black orb of smoke surrounding her body as dozens of guards appear out the shadows, walking towards us. Esmeralda pulls out two swords and runs towards us suddenly. I growl, stepping closer and ready to fight when Dagan grabs me. He throws me over his shoulder and takes off running the other way. I look back, pushing against Dagan as I see the guards drag Elias away into the shadows. My heart shatters and panic floods me.

"Let me go, what are you doing?" I demand, fighting him, but he is too strong. My dragon fights me, too, trying to make me shift, and my arms still burn from the cuts, knowing I couldn't fly even if I let her. *I can't save him.*

"Saving you. It is what Elias would want and

what has to happen. Tatarina is destroying the light, and you are all that is left," Dagan says harshly, and I turn in time to see Thorne slam his hands on the floor, making a large ice wall stretch up between us. The circular wall completely covers us, only leaving a small gap behind us to escape as we see Esmeralda slam her sword against the ice on the other side. Dagan holds me tightly as he darts through the gap, and I fight him, desperate to get back.

"Stop! Let me go! We can't leave him with her! She will kill him!" I cry as we run through the forest, following Melody.

"Doll, we don't have a choice! Do you think we want to leave him with her? No," Kor says from my left, and I growl at him. I catch Thorne's eyes for only a second, feeling his sorrow through our bond, but he still runs.

"I will hate you all if he dies, let me go!" I plead, my words turning into sobs.

"We are nearly at the portal," Melody shouts over her shoulder. Thorne and Kor shoot balls of ice and fire at guards that get near us. Dagan finally drops me and lets me go as we come to a stop, and Melody whispers to the portal we are at. I push him away as he tries to hold my hand, and he grabs my shoulders firmly, making me look at him.

"You would have frozen me if you truly believed you could save him. You can't, and you know it," Dagan says, wiping my tears away as he takes my hand. "She won't kill him, not when she can use him against you. If I thought there was any way to save my brother, I would be back there. We need to make a rescue plan, and we can do that on Earth. Okay?" he says, and I finally give up, even as it makes me sick to do so. One day on Earth to make a plan, that's it. She can't do too much to him in a day.

"Okay," I agree shakily, still hating that I can't run back now. I follow Melody through the portal back to Earth, knowing we will be back soon to get my dragon.

TWENTY-EIGHT

"A supermarket, great," Kor mutters as he comes through the portal last, and we stare around the empty place. Melody grabs a bottle of water off a shelf, opening it and drinking some before passing it to Kor.

"We should run, they could follow us," Kor says, accepting the drink. I just turn and stare at the portal, wishing Elias would run through it, escaping somehow.

"Is Bee okay?" I ask, glancing at her in Melody's arms. She looks less bright, less like Bee, and something isn't right.

"Earth isn't good for light spirits, and I don't know what Tatarina did back there," Melody says, looking both confused and worried at the same time. I have an idea, but not a good one.

"We will go back after we make a plan and clean up. Oh, and we need to get weapons," Dagan says, and I nod, walking through the aisle we have come out at.

"Is-o-la," Thorne strangles out my name, and I turn, seeing him holding his neck where a dart is sticking out of it. He falls to the floor as Dagan shouts out in a pain-filled grunt and drops to his knees. I grab him as he falls, pulling out the dart that is stuck in his neck and looking at it. *What the crap is that?*

"Run!" Kor demands, and I turn, only to stop as a figure walks down the aisle. I hear Kor and Melody fall behind me as Hallie steps into the light, holding a gun at me. She looks so different from the last time I saw her that I almost don't recognise her. Hallie's hair is up in a ponytail, the tips dyed a green colour that doesn't match her brown eyes that are narrowed on me. I look over her clothes, or outfit rather, that is black army gear or something. She is covered in guns, daggers, and there is even a sword on her back. *What happened to my friend?*

"Shoot her!" a man demands behind Hallie, and she holds a hand up as she focuses on me, and everything goes deadly silent. I can't help the brief smile I give her as I missed my friend, but I know something is wrong. They have done something to my dragons and sister.

"Isola," Hallie says coldly, and I hold my own hands up in surrender as she raises the gun higher.

"I don't understand. What are you doing? Hallie?" I ask her, and she shakes her head, holding the gun firm.

"My father told me what you are, but I didn't believe him! I didn't believe that monsters were real, and my best friend was one!" she shouts, locking her eyes with mine.

"I'm not a monster," I explain gently, seeing the five guys stepping behind her, wearing masks and holding their own guns up.

"My father hunts monsters like you, keeps us safe. You are a dragon, much like the monsters that took over Paris and destroyed it while you were gone! Thousands of people are dead or missing because of your people!" she spits out. "My mother was in Paris. My mother is gone, and it's all your fault!"

"I don't know anything about Paris!" I shout at her, getting frustrated. "I only want to save my own world. That is it."

"Same, and this is why I have to capture you and take you to my father. To the hunters' organisation," she says, her voice cracking as her hand shakes.

"You don't have to do this. You could let us go. I have to go back to Dragca for Elias, and I'm no threat to you. I'm your best friend, Hallie!" I plead, and I spot tears streaming down her face as she pulls the trigger, shooting a dart into my stomach. I hold my hands over it as I fall to my knees. She kneels down, too, looking straight into my eyes, and I can see nothing but hate reflecting back in them.

"You burnt down Michael's house and killed five teenagers. You are a monster and *not* my best friend. I clearly don't know you at all," she says, walking away. Everything gets blurry as I try to speak. I can only hear her footsteps on the floor as the world goes dark and one word leaves my lips.

"Eli."

EPILOGUE

ELIAS

"**E**lias Fire . . . you are so, so lucky," Tatarina taunts, grabbing my shoulder with her cold hand and digging her nails in as she smiles widely. I smirk before spitting in her face. She slams me back into a wall of the dungeon, my chains slamming against it as I stand up again.

"Kill me and get it over with, you bitch!" I shout. I close my eyes and picture only Isola. I feel content in the knowledge the others would have her safe on Earth by now.

"Death is not my plan for you. No. Isola will come for you, and when she does, I want her to know the pain of having the man she loves choose darkness over her," Tatarina says, chuckling to herself.

"I will never choose anything or anyone over Isola," I growl, opening my eyes again. Tatarina just smiles widely at my response.

"Darling, when I'm done, you won't even remember who she is," Tatarina laughs, holding her hand in the air, and a black cloud of smoke spreads from her hand.

"Isola," I shout as the smoke smothers me, and everything blurs away.

KEEP READING **book four by clicking here...**

ABOUT G. BAILEY

G. Bailey is a USA Today and international bestselling author of books that are filled with everything from dragons to pirates. Plus, fantasy worlds and breath-taking adventures.
G. Bailey is from the very rainy U.K. where she lives with her husband, two children, three cheeky dogs and one cat who rules them all.

(You can find exclusive teasers, random giveaways and sneak peeks of new books on the way in Bailey's Pack on Facebook or on TIKTOK— gbaileybooks)

FIND MORE BOOKS BY G. BAILEY ON AMAZON...

LINK HERE.

PART ONE
BONUS READ OF
THE MISSING WOLF

I'm Anastasia Noble, and shortly after moving to college, my life changed forever.

I became a familiar, bonded to a wolf for life and arrested simply for existing.

I woke up in the famous Familiar Empire community where I have to learn to bond with my wolf, or I can never leave.

Never again see those whom I love.

Bonding is my only option, if you could even call it an option, but add in familiars going missing every week, plus being stuck in a cabin with three mysterious, attractive, male familiars and their maddening animals...*this is not going to be easy.*

17+ RH

THE MISSING WOLF

LEAVING THE PAST BEHIND.

ANASTASIA

I stand still on the side of the train tracks, letting the cold wind blow my blonde and purple dip-dyed hair across my face. I squeeze the handle of my suitcase tighter, hoping that the train will come soon. *It's freezing today, and my coat is packed away in the suitcase, dammit.* I feel like I've waited for this day for years, the day I get to leave my foster home and join my sister at college. I look behind me into the parking lot, seeing my younger sister stood watching me go, my foster grandmother holding her hand. Phoebe is only eleven years old, but she is acting strong today, no matter how much she wants me to stay. I smile at her, trying to ignore how difficult it feels to leave her here, but I know she couldn't be in a better home. I can get through college with our older sister and then get a job in the city, while living all together. *That's the plan anyway.*

We lost our mum and dad in a car accident ten years ago, and we were more than lucky to find a foster parent that would take all three of us in. Grandma Pops is a special kind of lady. She is kind and loves to cook, and the money she gets from fostering pays for her house. She lost her two children in a fire years ago, and she tells us regularly that we keep her happy and alive. Even if we do eat a lot for three kids. Luckily, she likes to look after us as I burn everything I attempt to cook. And I don't even want to remember the time I tried to wash my clothes, which ended in disaster.

"Train four-one-nine to Liverpool is calling at the station in one minute," the man announces over the loudspeaker, just before I hear the sound of the train coming in from a distance. I turn back to see the grey train speeding towards us, only slowing down when it gets close, but I still have to walk to get to the end carriage. I wait for the two men in front of me to get on before I step onto the carriage, turning to pull my suitcase on. I search through the full seats until I find an empty one near the back, next to a window. I have to make sure it's facing the way the train is going as it freaks me out to sit the other way. I slide my suitcase under the seat before sitting down, leaving my handbag on the small table in front of me.

I wave goodbye to my sister, who waves back, her head hidden on grandma's shoulder as she cries. I can only see her waist length, wavy blonde hair before the train pulls away. I'm going to miss her. *Urgh, it's not like we don't have phones and FaceTime!* I'm being silly. I pull my phone out of my bag and quickly send a message to my older sis, letting her know I am on the train. I also send a message to Phoebe, telling her how much I love and miss her already.

"Ticket?" the train employee guy asks, making me jump out of my skin, and my phone falls on the floor.

"Sorry! I'm always dropping stuff," I say, and the man just stares at me with a serious expression, still holding his hand out. His uniform is crisply ironed, and his hair is combed to the left without a single hair out of place. I roll my eyes and pull my bag open, pulling out my ticket and handing it to him. After he checks it for about a minute, he scribbles on it before handing it back to me. I've never understood why they bother drawing on the tickets when the machines check the tickets at the other end anyway. I put my ticket back into my bag before sliding it under the seat just as the train moves, jolting me a little.

I reach for my phone, which is stuck to some paper underneath it. I've always been taught to pick up rubbish, so I grab the paper as well as my phone before slipping out from under the table and back to my seat. I put my phone back into my handbag before looking at the leaflet I've picked up. It's one of those warning leaflets about familiars and how it is illegal to hide one. The leaflet has a giant lion symbol at the top and warning signs around the edges. It explains that you have to call the police and report them if you find one.

Familiars account for 0.003 percent of the human race, though many say they are nothing like humans and don't like to count them as such. Familiars randomly started appearing about fifty years ago, or at least publicly they did. A lot of people believe they just kept themselves hidden before that. The Familiar Empire was soon set up, and it is the only place safe for familiars to live in peace. They have their own laws, an alliance with humans, and their own land in Scotland, Spain and North America.

Unfortunately, anyone could suddenly become a familiar, and you wouldn't know until one random day. It can be anything from a car crash to simply waking up that sets off the gene, but once a familiar, always a familiar. They have the mark on their hand, a glowing tattoo of whatever animal is bonded to them. The animals are the main reason familiars are so dangerous. They have a bond with one animal who would do anything for them. Even kill. And I heard once that some kid's animal was a lion as big as an elephant. But those are just the things we know publicly, who knows what is hidden behind the giant walls of the Familiar Empire?

"My uncle is one, you know?" a girl says, and I look up to see a young girl about ten years old hanging over her seat, her head tilted to the side as she stares at the leaflet in my hand. "He has a big rabbit for a familiar."

"That's awesome..." I say, smiling as I put the leaflet down. I bet picking up giant rabbit poo isn't that awesome, but I don't tell her that.

"I want to be a familiar when I grow up," she

excitedly says. "They have cool powers and pets! Mum won't even let me get a dog!"

"Sit down, Clara! Stop talking to strangers!" her mum says, tugging the girl's arm, and she sits down after flashing me a cheeky grin.

I fold the leaflet and slide it into my bag before resting back in the seat, watching the city flash by from the window. I couldn't think of anything worse than being a familiar. You have to leave your family, your whole life, and live in the woods. *Being a familiar seems like nothing but a curse.*

Keep reading here...

THE MISSING WOLF

WHO WEARS A CLOAK THESE DAYS?

"Ana!!" my sister practically screeches as I step off the train, and then throws herself at me before I get a second to really look at her. Even though my sister is only a few inches taller than my five-foot-four self, she nearly knocks me over. I pull her blonde hair away from my face as it tries to suffocate me before she thankfully pulls away. I'm not a hugger, but Bethany always ignores that little fact.

"I missed you too, Bethany," I mutter, and she grins at me. Bethany was always the beautiful sister, and as we got older, she just got prettier. Seems the year at college has only added to that. Her blonde hair is almost white, falling in perfect waves down her back. Mine is the same, but I dyed the ends a deep purple. Another one of my attempts at sticking out in a crowd when I usually become invisible next to my gorgeous sister. Phoebe is the image of Bethany, and both of them look like photos of our mother. Whereas I look like my dad mostly, I still have the blonde hair. Bethany grins at me, then slowly runs her eyes over my outfit before letting out a long sigh.

"You look so pretty, sis," she says, and I roll my eyes. Bethany hates jeans and long-sleeved tops, which I happen to be wearing both. I didn't even look at what I threw on this morning. I shiver as the cold wind blows around me, reminding me that I should have gotten my coat out my suitcase on the train trip. It is autumn.

"You're such a bad liar," I reply, arching an eyebrow at her, and she laughs.

"Well, you are eighteen now, and I've never seen you in a dress. College is going to change all that." She waves a hand like she has sorted all the problems out.

"How so? I'm not wearing a dress to classes," I say, frowning at her. "Leggings are much easier to run around in, I think."

"Parties, of course," she tuts, laughing like it

should be obvious. Bethany grabs hold of my suitcase before walking down the now empty sidewalk to the parking lot at the end.

"I need to study. There is no way I'm going to ace my nursing classes without a lot of studying," I tell her. Bethany took drama, and I wasn't the least bit surprised when she was offered a job at the end of her course, depending on her grades. Though she was an A-star student throughout high school, so there is no way she could fail.

"I love that you will have the same job mum did," she eventually tells me, and I glance over at her as she smiles sadly at me before focusing back on where she is walking. I remember my mum and dad, whereas Bethany is just over one year older than me and remembers a lot more. Phoebe doesn't remember them at all; she only has our photos and the things we can tell her. It was difficult for Bethany to leave us both to come to college, but grandma and I told her she had to find a future.

"I doubt I will do it as well as her...but I like to help people. I know this is the right thing for me to do," I reply, and I see her nod in the corner of my eye. I quickly walk forward and hold the metal gate to the car park open for Bethany to walk through before catching up with her as we walk past cars.

"You've always been the nice one. I remember when you were twelve, and the boy down the road broke up with you because some other girl asked him out. The next day, that boy fell off his bike, cutting all his leg just outside our home. You helped him into the house, put plasters on his leg, and then walked his bike back to his house for him," she remarks. "Most people wouldn't have done that. I would have just laughed at him before leaving him on the sidewalk."

"I also called him a dumbass," I say, laughing at the memory of his shocked face. "So I wasn't all that nice."

"That's why you are so amazing, sis," she laughs, and I chuckle as we get to Bethany's car. It's a run down, black Ford Fiesta, but I know Bethany adores the old thing. Even if there are scratches and bumps all over the poor car from Bethany's terrible driving.

"Get in, I can put the suitcase in the boot," she says, and I pull the passenger door open before sliding inside. I do my seatbelt up before resting back, watching out of the passenger window at the train pulling out of the station. There is a man in a black cloak stood still in the middle of the path, the wind pushing his cloak around his legs, but his hood is up, covering his face. I just stare, feeling stranger and more freaked out by the second as the man lifts his head. I see a flash of yellow under his hood for a brief moment, and I sit forward, trying to see more of the strange man I can't pull my eyes from. I almost jump out of my skin when Bethany gets in the car, slamming her door shut behind her, and I look over at her.

"Are you okay? You look pale," she asks, reaching over to put her hand on my head to check my temperature before pulling it away. I look back towards the man, seeing that he and the train are gone. Everything is quiet, still and creepy. *Time to go.*

"Yeah, everything is fine. I'm just nervous about my first day," I tell her, which is sort of honest, but I'm missing the little fact about the weird hooded man. *I mean, who walks around in cloaks like friggin' Darth Vader?* She frowns at me, seeing through my lies easily, but after I don't say a word for a while, she drops it.

"It will be fine. Don't worry!" she says, reaching over to squeeze my hand before starting the car. I keep my eyes on the spot the man was in until I can't see it anymore. I close my eyes and shake my head, knowing it was just a creepy guy, and I need to forget it. This is my first day of my new life, and nothing is going to ruin that.

THE MISSING WOLF

ONE MOMENT CAN CHANGE EVERYTHING.

"Anastasia Noble?" I hear someone shout out as I wait in the middle of the crowd of new students. Bethany left me here about half an hour ago, and she is going to find me later once I have my room sorted. First, I have to get through a tour of the university, even though I had a tour here when I visited two months ago. I also spent days studying the map they gave me, so I know where I am going. Putting my hand in the air, I move through the crowd, pulling my suitcase behind me with my arm starting to ache from lugging the giant purple suitcase everywhere.

I get to the front of the crowd, where an older man waves me over. I quickly make my way to him and the three other students waiting at his side. Two of them are girls, both blonde and whispering between themselves with their pink suitcases. The other is a guy who is too interested in ogling the blondes to notice me coming over. Story of my life right there. I stop right in front of the older man who stinks of too much cologne, and I shake his slightly sweaty hand before stepping back.

"Welcome to Liverpool University. We are the smallest, but fiercest, university in northern England. Now, I am going to show you around the basic area before taking you to your rooms. You all will share a corridor and living area, so look around at your new friends and maybe say hello!" the man says, clapping his hands together before quickly turning to walk away. We all jog to catch up with him as he walks us across the grass towards one of the buildings on either side of the clearing.

There is a little river in the middle with planted flowers and trees all surrounding it. It's peaceful, exactly why my sister chose this university, I suspect. She always likes seeing the beauty in life, where I am always looking for a way to fix the world instead. I wish we had other family around that could tell us about what our parents were like, who each of us follow, or if we are just random in the family line of personalities. We don't even know if our parents had any close friends. There is nothing much in our foster pack given to grandma from social services. Bethany and I talked about going to the village we lived in to ask around, but neither of us ever found the time.

"Anastasia, right?" a guy asks, slowing down to walk at my side. He has messy brown hair, blue eyes, and a big rucksack on his back.

"Yep, who are you?" I ask.

"Don. Nice to meet you," he replies, offering me a hand to shake with a big grin. I shake his hand before looking up at the massive archway we are walking through to get inside of the building. It is two smooth pillars meeting together in the middle. There are old gargoyle statues lining the archway, their creepy eyes staring down at me. Those statues always creep me out. Bethany thinks it's funny, so last Christmas, she got me gargoyle romance books as a joke. Jokes on her though; some of those books were damn good. I quickly look away, back to where we are walking, as Don starts talking again.

"I've heard there is a party tonight to welcome freshers. Are you going?" he asks me, his arm annoyingly brushing against mine with how closely he has decided to walk. I glance up at him to see his gaze is firmly focused on my breasts rather than my face.

"No. I need to unpack," I curtly reply.

"Can't it wait one night?" he asks, and I look over at him once again. He is gorgeous, but the whiney attitude about a party is a big turn off. "I will make sure you have fun."

"No. It can't wait, and I doubt anything you could do would make the party fun for me," I say honestly, and not shockingly, he nods before catching up with the two blonde girls in the group, trying his pickup techniques on them. *Men.*

Bethany says I'm picky, but actually, it's just because the general male population at my age are idiots and act like kids most of the time too. I don't see how anyone could want to date them, though Bethany is on her twelfth boyfriend since she came to college, so I know she doesn't share my opinion. She swears she will know when the right guy comes along, and it will be the same for me. I doubt it. Anyway, finding the "right" guy is not the most important thing at the moment; passing college and getting my nursing degree is.

"This is the oldest part of the university and where most the lessons are. In the welcome packs sent to your old homes were the links to an app which is a map. It will help you find your lessons," the tour guide explains before opening a door out of the old corridor and into another one which is more modern. There are white-tiled floors, lockers lining the walls, and spotlights in the ceiling that shine so brightly everything gleams. "Every student gets a locker here, which is perfect for storing books and anything you don't need for every class. Trust me, you will get a lot of books, so the lockers are a godsend."

We walk down the corridor, listening to the guide explain the history of the university when suddenly there is a burning feeling in my hand that comes out of nowhere. I scream, dropping to my knees as I grab my hand, trying to stop the incredible pain. I rub at my pale skin as it burns hot, yet there is nothing there to see. The pain gets worse until I can't see or hear anything for a moment, and I fall back. When I blink my eyes open, I'm lying on the cold floor, hearing the chatter of students near me. No one is helping me, oddly enough, and they sound like they are far away. Every part of my body hurts, aches like I've been running a marathon.

"She's a familiar. Has anyone called the police?" one person asks as I stare up at the flickering spotlight right above me.

"We should leave; she could hurt us. Who knows where her creature is!" another man harshly whispers. I lift my hand above my face almost in slow motion. My eyes widen in pure shock at the huge, glowing, purple wolf tattoo covering the back of my hand where it burned. It stops at my wrist, the wolf's fur extending halfway up my fingers and thumb. The eyes of the wolf tattoo glow the brightest as I realise what this means.

"I'm a familiar."

THE MISSING WOLF

TIME TO RUN BEFORE IT IS TOO LATE.

As soon as I've said it out loud, it feels like I can't breathe as I sit up and look around at the people staring at me. The group I was with are huddled by the lockers a good distance away from me now, and I turn to see more people have shown up, a few of them on their phones. All of them are scared, worried what I will do as they keep their eyes on me. They are going to call the police and have me taken away because of this. *I have to get to Bethany first.* I have to at least say goodbye to her before they come for me and take me some place where I may never see her again.

I quickly scramble to my feet and run down the corridor, passing everyone who shouts for me to stop, until I get to the door at the end. I push it open, running through the arch and into the empty clearing. Stopping by the river, I look up and quickly try to remember how to get to the dorms. Shit, I don't even know what room she is in. I pull my handbag off my shoulder to get my phone out just as I hear a low growl from right behind me.

I slowly drop my bag onto the floor and turn around, seeing a giant wolf inches away from my face. The wolf is taller than I am; its head is leant down so I can see into its stunning blue eyes. They remind me of my own eyes, to be honest, with little swirls of black, light and dark blues, all mixed together. My body and mind seem to relax as I stare at the creature, one which I should be terrified of... but I am not. I feel myself moving my hand up, and then the wolf growls a little, shaking me out of that thought.

I step back, which only seems to piss her or him off more. Some deep part of me knows I have to touch the wolf now, or I will always regret it. I take a deep breath before stepping closer and quickly placing my hand on the middle of the wolf's forehead. I didn't notice it was my hand with the familiar mark on it until this point, until it glows so brightly purple that I have to turn my head away. When the light dims, I look back to see the black wolf staring at me as I lower my hand.

"Your name is Shadow," I say out loud, though I don't have a clue how I know that, but I know it is true. Shadow bows his head before lying on the ground in front of me. He is my familiar. *That's how I know.* That's why I am not scared of the enormous wolf like I should be. I have a gigantic wolf for my familiar. *Holy crap.* It takes me a few seconds to pull my gaze from Shadow and remember what I was going to do. Find my sister, that's what.

"We need to find my sister...can you help me? Like smell her, maybe? She smells like me," I ask Shadow and then realise I have no clue if he can understand me. Shadow looks up, tilting his head to the side before stretching out, knocking his head into my stomach. I step back, sighing. "Never mind."

Shadow growls at me, and I give him a questioning look. What is up with the growling? I thought familiar animals were meant to be familiars' best friends or something. I really get the feeling Shadow isn't all that impressed with me. He shakes his giant head before walking around me and slowly running off in the direction of the other building.

"Wait up!" I have to run fast to catch up with him as he gets to the front of the university, people moving fast out of his way and some even screaming. I don't even blame them. A giant black wolf running towards you is not something you see every day. I run faster, getting to Shadow's side as we round a corner, and I hear Bethany's laugh just before I see her sat on a bench with a guy. They both turn with wide, scared eyes to us, and the guy falls back off the bench before running away.

The sounds of people's screaming, shouting and general fear drift into nothing but silence as I meet my sister's eyes as she stands up. A tear streams down her cheek, saying everything neither one of us can speak. I will be made to leave her, and I have no idea when—if ever—I will get to see her again. Bethany is the first to move, running to me and wrapping her arms around my shoulders. She doesn't even look at Shadow; she doesn't fear me either, which is a huge relief. I hug her back, trying to commit every part of her to my memory as I try not to cry. *I have to be strong.* If I break down now,

Bethany will never be able to cope. I pull back as I hear sirens in the background and know my time here is coming to an end.

"I will find a way back to you. I will never stop until I do. Just look after yourself and Phoebe. Promise me?" I ask Bethany, holding my hands on her shoulders as she sobs.

"I promise. If anyone can work out a way around the rules, it's you. I love you, sis," she says, crying her eyes out between each word. I hug her once more before stepping back to Shadow's side, away from my sister and my old life. "Be safe."

"Go. Just go, I don't want you to see me arrested or how nasty the police are to familiars. The YouTube videos are enough," I say, but Bethany shakes her head, wiping her cheeks and crossing her arms. I've accidently seen enough videos online to know that the police, the government and the general population are not nice to new familiars. That's why they are taken straight away. I'm not going to fight or try to run like some familiars do. I doubt I would get far with Shadow at my side.

"I am staying until they take you. You will not be alone," she says as I hear shouting and the sounds of dozens of feet running towards us. I gasp as I feel a sharp prick in the side of my neck, and Bethany screams. Shadow growls, which turns into a howl as I try to reach for him as he falls to the ground at my side. The world turns to blackness, and the last thing I hear is Bethany's pleas for someone to leave me alone.

THE MISSING WOLF

NEW LIFE. NEW WORLD.

I cough as I wake up, my throat feeling dry and scratchy as I look up at the wood ceiling above me. The smell of fire and smoke fills my nose, making me lift my hand to rub it as I sit up. A red blanket falls to my lap as I look around the cabin I am in. Shadow is lying on the floor near a window, his eyes watching me closely, and the rest of the room is just a row of beds like the one I am in. There is a fireplace on the far wall, where the smell of burning wood is coming from. I look out the window Shadow is lying under, seeing frost covered trees. It wasn't frosty in Liverpool the last time I checked. Where have they taken me? Surely, I haven't slept the entire way to the Familiar Empire...but the evidence is looking like that is likely.

I slip my legs out of the bed, seeing that I'm still wearing the clothes from my first day at university, but they are wrinkled now, and the jeans are dirty with mud. There is a glass of water on the bedside unit and a little note. I pick the water up and take a sip before drinking it all quickly once I realise how thirsty I am. I put the glass down and pick up the note, hastily reading it.

Welcome to your new home, the Familiar Empire.
The door by the fireplace leads to a bathroom, and a spare outfit is in there for you from your suitcase. Clean up and come outside. R.

I put the note back down and stare over at Shadow, remembering Bethany's pleas before the police—I presume—knocked me out. There is no going back now. I'm a familiar, and my life as I knew it is over. Grandma Pops always said you have to make the best of a bad situation because giving up is not an option. That is what I am going to do. I can fix this...*somehow*. I slide off the bed, walking past Shadow, who watches my every movement before getting to the door near the fireplace. I push it and walk inside, closing the door behind me.

The bathroom smells of bleach, but I guess that means it's clean at least. It's colder in here, and its basic design is something you would see in any hotel. There is a shower, towels on a shelf nearby, and a standard toilet and sink. I quickly use the toilet before washing my hands and looking around for the clothes. On a wooden laundry box in the corner is a pile of clothes, as the note mentioned. I pick them up, seeing ripped jeans and a blue jumper. This is one of my favourite jumpers, so I'm glad they picked that, especially considering the frost covered trees outside. I mentally catalogue all the clothes I have in my suitcase and know that not a lot of them are suitable for cold weather. I had saved up money for college, and there was little else left. Plus, Bethany assured me she had winter clothes I could borrow. *Dammit.* There is also a pink bra and matching knickers under the pile. I don't want to know who went through my suitcase and picked these; I can only hope it was a girl. By the simple fact they are a matching set, I'm willing to bet it was.

I put the clothes back and carefully pull off my dirt covered clothes. I leave them all in a pile by the sink, and as I glance up, I see my reflection in the small mirror. My hair is messy, sticking in all directions, and my skin is pale. There are big bags under my eyes, even though I've clearly slept for a long time, and my blue eyes now only remind me of Shadow and how similar they are.

I grip the sink, looking down and breathing in deep breaths. I'm a familiar. I wish I had learnt more about their kind growing up, but I never suspected I would be one of them. Only 0.003 percent of the entire human race are. *What are the chances I would be one of them?* I breathe in and shake my head once again. I know I need to shower and face the world I am now a part of. I only have to make my shaky legs move first.

It takes a few seconds before I can let go of the sink and walk the few steps to the shower. I step back as I switch it on, knowing there is a good chance cold water is going to come out first. Knowing me, I'd end up jumping back and knocking myself out somehow. I put my hand out and test the water, waiting for it to go warm before finally stepping in. Resting my head under the warm water, I let it soothe me before opening my eyes, seeing hotel-like little bottles on a shelf in front of me. I'm curious about this place, so I quickly wash my hair and myself before getting out the shower.

Lacking a hair dryer and my brush, I towel dry my hair as much as possible before running my fingers through it. It feels good to pull my clean clothes on, and I fold the towels up, not wanting to leave a mess. Going back to the mirror, I glance at myself one more time, knowing I need to walk out of here with my head lifted high. I'm Anastasia Noble, and I am familiar. The more I repeat it, the more it sinks in. This is my life now.